W9-CIC-498

William Carlos Williams
THE DOCTOR STORIES

By William Carlos Williams

William Carlos Williams
THE DOCTOR STORIES

Compiled with an introduction by Robert Coles, M.D.

Afterword by William Eric Williams, M.D.

A   N E W   D I R E C T I O N S   B O O K

BROOKLINE PUBLIC LIBRARY

copy 1

3 1712 00535 3407

Copyright © 1932, 1933, 1934, 1937, 1938, 1941, 1943, 1947, 1948, 1949, 1950, 1951, 1962 by William Carlos Williams
Introduction copyright © 1984 by Robert Coles
Afterword copyright © 1983 by William Eric Williams

All rights reserved. Except for brief passages quoted in a newspaper, magazine, radio, or television review, no part of this book may be reproduced in any form or by any means, electronic or mechanical, including photocopying and recording, or by any information storage and retrieval system, without permission in writing from the Publisher.

William Eric Williams's essay, "My Father, the Doctor," first appeared in *New Directions in Prose and Poetry 47* and in the William Carlos Williams Commemorative Issue of the *Journal of the Medical Society of New Jersey*. A different version of the poem, "The Birth," was first published in the Winter 1962 issue of the *Massachusetts Review* but neither variant appears in any collection of Williams's poems.

Manufactured in the United States of America
First published clothbound and as New Directions Paperbook 585 in 1984
Published simultaneously in Canada by George J. McLeod, Ltd., Toronto

Library of Congress Cataloging in Publication Data

Williams, William Carlos, 1883–1963.
   The doctor stories.
   (A New Directions Book)
   1. Physicians—Fiction.   I. Coles, Robert.
II. Title.
PS3545.I544A6   1984   813'.52   84-8372
ISBN 0-8112-0925-3
ISBN 0-8112-0926-1 (pbk.)

New Directions Books are published for James Laughlin
by New Directions Publishing Corporation,
80 Eighth Avenue, New York 10011

Contents

Introduction

A GREAT PRIVILEGE (and actually, turn of fate) befell me in the early 1950s, when I was encouraged by a fine professor-friend of mine, under whose supervision I'd written my undergraduate thesis, to send a note to William Carlos Williams and ask him whether he'd mind reading a college student's effort to understand his poetry, especially the first book of *Paterson*. This inquiry was not thoroughly gratuitous or self-serving, Professor Perry Miller kept insisting— a response to my fearful hesitancy, an attitude which surely (I now realize) protected me from realizing how much of my pride, if not (as today's psychiatrists call it) narcissism had been put into that research and writing effort. This particular poet, Mr. Miller reminded me several times, was hardly a favorite of many college professors, and might well enjoy reading what a student writing in an ivy-covered dormitory library managed to say about *Paterson*, wherein no huge flowering of ivy is recorded.

Soon enough, I'd dispatched my essay, and received a warm, friendly and lively response to it, coupled with an invitation to drop by; and soon enough I did. For me, to know Dr. Williams, to hear him talk about his writing and his life of medical work among the poor and working people of northern New Jersey, was to change direction markedly. Once headed for teaching, I set my sights for medical school. The result was a fairly rough time with both the pre-medical courses, not easy for me, and medical school itself, where I had a lot of trouble figuring out what kind of doctoring I'd be able to do with a modest amount of competence. During those years, ailing though Dr. Williams was, he found the time and energy to give me several much needed boosts—as in this comment: "Look, you're not out on a four-year picnic at that medical school, so stop talking like a disappointed lover. You signed up for a spell of training and they're dishing it out to you, and all you can do is take everything they've got, everything they hand to you, and tell yourself how lucky you are to be on the receiving end—so you can be a doctor, and that's no bad price to pay for the worry, the exhaustion."

Anyone who knew him would recognize the familiar way of putting things, of approaching both another person and this life's hurdles: kind and understanding underneath, but bluntly practical and unsentimental. Not that Williams didn't have in him (and in his writing) a wonderful romanticism, an ardently subjective willingness to take big risks with his mind and heart. His greatest achievement, *Paterson*, is a lyrical examination of a given city's social history, from the early days of this country to the middle of the twentieth century—and the poet whose eyes and ears become the reader's is marvellously vibrant, daring. But there is also in that poem, and in other aspects of Williams' work a sensible and skeptical voice—the side of Williams these stories reveal to us: a hard working doctor whose flights of fancy are always being curbed by a sharp awareness of exactly what life demands as well as offers.

I will never forget an exchange I had with Williams when I was in my last year of medical school. He had been sick rather a lot by then, but his feisty spirit was still in evidence, and as well, his canny ability to appraise a situation—anyone or anything—quickly and accurately. I told him I wanted to take a residency in pediatrics. He said "fine," then looked right into my eyes and addressed me this way: "I know you'll like the kids. They'll keep your spirits high. But can you go after them—grab them and hold them down and stick needles in them and be deaf to their noise?" Oh yes, I could do that. Well, he wasn't so sure. Mind you, he wasn't being rudely personal with me. He was just talking as the old man he was, who had seen a lot of patients, and yes, a lot of doctors, too. "Give yourself more time," he urged me, in conclusion. Then he regaled me with some (literally speaking) "doctor stories"—accounts of various colleagues of his: how they did their various jobs; the joys some of them constantly experienced, or alas, the serious troubles a number of them had struggled to overcome; the satisfactions of x, y, z specialties, and conversely, the limitations of those same specialties. It was a discourse, a grand tour of sorts, and I remember to this day the contours of that lively exchange. I told my advisor at medical school about the meeting, and I can still recall those words, too: "You're lucky to know him."

We are all lucky to know him, to have him in our continuing midst. Only in those last years of his life was William Carlos Williams, finally, obtaining the recognition he'd failed to receive for many decades of a brilliantly original, productive literary life. But during that early spell of relative critical neglect (or outright dismissal, or patronizing half-notice) this particular writer could rely upon other sources of approval. Every day of a long medical life (and often enough, in the middle of the night, too) he was called by the men, women and children of northern New Jersey, ordinary people, plain people who considered themselves lucky to hold a job, lucky to be able to get by, barely, or not so lucky, because jobless—families who had one very important loyalty in common, no matter their backgrounds, and they were ethnically diverse: a willingness, an eagerness, a downright determination to consider one Rutherford doctor their doctor, W. C. Williams, M.D. We who think of poets often look wide and far for their spiritual roots, their cultural moorings. William Carlos Williams was one poet who made quite clear who his teachers were, where they lived, how they affected him, helped shape his particular sensibility: "Yet there is/ no return: rolling up out of chaos,/ a nine months' wonder, the city/ the man, an identity—it can't be/ otherwise—an/ interpenetration, both ways."

The city was, of course, Paterson, the Paterson of *Pater-*

son, the Paterson of industrial strife, of smokestacks and foundries and assembly lines, the Paterson of foreign languages still native tongues, of Italians and Jews and Poles and the Irish and the Blacks, the Paterson of desperately poor people in the 1930s, part of that enormous nation within a nation characterized by Franklin Delano Roosevelt in 1933 as "ill-fed, ill-housed and ill-clothed." As the poet of Paterson declared, he had struggled himself in that city of hard-pressed souls, and so doing, had become very much part of a given human scene—not only the lyric observer or prophet, as in *Paterson* of five epic volumes, but also the obstetrician and gynecologist, the school doctor, the pediatrician, the general practitioner: the young doc and the middle-aged doc and the old doc who drove all over and walked all over and climbed steps all over Paterson (and Rutherford and other New Jersey towns), a family legend to hundreds and hundreds rather than a literary giant (eventually) to hundreds and hundreds of thousands.

"Outside/ outside myself/ there is a world," the poet of *Paterson* declares himself to have "rumbled," and then notes that such a world was "subject" to his "incursions," and was one he made it his business to "approach concretely." No question he did, with all the directness, earthiness, and urgent immediacy of a doctor who knows life itself to be at stake—someone else's, and in a way (professional, moral) his own as well. I remember the doctor describing his work, telling stories that were real events, wondering in retrospect how he did it, kept going at such a pace, hauled himself so many miles a day, got himself up so many stairs, persisted so long and hard with families who had trouble, often enough, using English, never mind paying their bills. And as he knew, and sometimes had to say out loud, even mention in his writing, it wasn't as if he was loaded with money, or a writer who took in big royalties.

America's Depression was a disaster for Dr. Williams' patients, and many of them never paid him much, if indeed, anything at all. America's Depression was also a time when a marvelously versatile, knowing, and gifted writer who happened to be a full-time doctor was not having any great success with critics, especially the powerful ones who claimed for themselves the imprimatur of the academy. No wonder this writing doctor was glad to go "outside" himself, greet and try to comprehend a world other than that of literary people. No wonder, too, he shunned the possibility of a relatively plush Manhattan practice—the doctor to well-known cultural figures. His patients may have been obscure, down and out, even illiterate by the formal testing standards of one or another school system, but they were, he had figured out early on, a splendidly vital people—full of important experiences to tell, memories to recall, ideas to try on their most respected of visitors, the busy doc who yet could be spellbound by what he chanced to hear, and knew to keep in mind at night when the typewriter replaced the stethoscope as his major professional instrument.

I remember asking Williams the usual, dreary question— one I hadn't stopped to realize he'd been asked a million or so times before: how did he do it, manage two full-time careers so well and for so long? His answer was quickly forthcoming, and rendered with remarkable tact and patience, given the provocation: "It's no strain. In fact, the one [medicine] nourishes the other [writing], even if at times I've groaned to the contrary." If he had sometimes complained that he felt drained, overworked, denied the writing time he craved, needed, he would not forget for long all the sustaining, healing, inspiring moments a profession—a calling, maybe, it was in his life—had given him: moment upon moment in the course of more than four decades of medical work.

Such moments are the stuff of these "doctor stories"—the best of their kind since Dr. Anton Chekhov did his (late nineteenth-century) storytelling. As one goes through Williams' evocation of a twentieth-century American medical practice, the sheer daring of the literary effort soon enough comes to mind—the nerve he had to say what he says. These are brief talks, or accounts meant to register disappointment, frustration, confusion, perplexity; or, of course, enchantment, pleasure, excitement, strange or surprising or simple and not at all surprising satisfaction. These are stories that tell of mistakes, of errors of judgment; and as well, of one modest breakthrough, then another—not in research efforts of major clinical projects, but in that most important of all situations, the would-be healer face-to-face with the sufferer who half desires, half dreads the stranger's medical help. As I heard Dr. Williams once say: "Even when the patients knew me well, and trusted me a lot, I could sense their fear, their skepticism. And why not? I could sense my own worries, my own doubts!"

He has the courage to share in these stories such raw and usually unacknowledged turmoil with his readers—even as he took after himself in an almost Augustinian kind of self-scrutiny toward the end of the second book of *Paterson*. In almost every story the doctor is challenged not only by his old, familiar antagonist, disease, but that other foe whose continuing power is a given for all of us—pride in all its forms, disguises, assertions. It is this "unreflecting egoism," as George Eliot called it, which the doctor-narrator of these stories allows us to see, and so doing, naturally, we are nudged closer to ourselves. Narcissism, as we of this era have learned to call the sin of pride, knows no barriers of race or class—of occupation or profession, either. But as ministers and doctors occasionally realize, there is a sad, inevitable irony at work in their lives—the preacher flawed in precisely the respect he denounces during his sermons, the doctor ailing even as he tries to heal others.

Williams knew the special weakness we all have for those who have a moral hold on us, for those who attend us in our life-and-death times. Williams knew, too, that such a vulnerability prompts gullibility, an abject surrender of one's personal authority—and the result is not only the jeopardy of the parishioner or the patient, but the priest or the physician. Arrogance is the other side of eager acquiescence. Presumptuousness and self-importance are the wounds this life imposes upon those privy to the wounds of others. The busy, capable doctor, well aware of all the burdens he must carry, and not in the least inclined to shirk his duties, may stumble badly in those small moral moments that constantly press upon him or her—the nature of a hello or good-bye, the tone of voice as a question is asked or answered, the private thoughts one has, and the effect they have on our face, our hands as they do their work, our posture, our gait. "There's nothing like a difficult patient to show us ourselves," Williams once said to a medical student, and then he expanded the observation further: "I would learn so much on my rounds, or making home visits. At times I felt like a thief because I heard words, lines, saw people and places—and used it all in my writing. I guess I've told people that, and no one's so surprised! There was something deeper going on, though—the *force* of all those encounters. I was put off guard again and again, and the result was—well, a descent into myself."

He laughed as he said that, and worried about a comparison he nevertheless proceeded to make—with the achievement of "insight" in psychoanalysis. I say "worried" because he knew rather well that he had in mind a moral as well as psychological or emotional confrontation, and he'd been hearing a lot in those last years of his life (to his amazement and chagrin) about a supposedly "value-free" psychoanalysis or social science. Not that he couldn't put aside his anger and disgust and simply laugh at his own pretensions and spells of blindness, at those of others. These stories abound with such self-mocking gestures—parody turned on the parodist, words used to take the stern (but also compassionate) measure of the doctor who dispensed (among other things) words, and then went home to dish them out—well, "in the American grain." It is important to emphasize the humorous and tolerant side of this storytelling self-arraignment of a singular New Jersey doctor: even the terribly hurt, driven, melancholy "Old Doc Rivers" is not without his spirited decency—a dizzying mix of selfless honor, passionate concern, and alas, the unrestrained demonic constantly at work.

These stories are, really, frank confidences extended to the rest of us by one especially knowing, dedicated physician who was willing to use his magical gifts of storytelling in a gesture of—what? We all require forgiveness, and we all hope to redeem our own missteps—hope, through whatever grace is granted us, to make every possible reparation. Words were the instrument of grace given to this one doctor, and words are the instrument of grace, also, for the rest of us, the readers who have and will come upon these marvelously provocative tales. As Dr. Williams' beloved wife Flossie (she appears now and then in these medical fictions) once said to me: "There's little in a doctor's life Bill didn't get at when he wrote." She'd been there with him, of course, all along, and she knew: the periods of irritability and impatience; the flashes of annoyance and resentment; the instance of greed, or just plain bitterness that "they" can't, don't, won't pay up; the surge of affection—even desire, lust; the assertion of power—a fierce wish to control, to tell in no uncertain terms, to win at all costs; the tiredness, the exhaustion, the despondency. The rush of it all, the fast-paced struggle, again and again, with all sorts of illnesses—and the victories over them, the defeats at their hands, and not least, the realization (postmortem) of one's limitations, one's mistakes.

For years I have been teaching these doctor stories to medical students, and during each class we all seem newly awakened—encouraged to ask the important whys, consider the perplexing ifs. The stories offer medical students and their teachers an opportunity to discuss the big things, so to speak, of the physician's life—the great unmentionables that are, yet, everyday aspects of doctoring: the prejudices we feel (and feel ashamed of), the moments of spite or malice we try to overlook, the ever loaded question of money, a matter few of us like to discuss, yet one constantly stirring us to pleasure, to bedeviling disappointment in others, in ourselves. What, in fact, that is really important has Williams left out? Nothing, it seems. He gives us a chance to discuss the alcoholic doctor, the suicidal doctor. He prompts us to examine our ambitions, our motives, our aspirations, our purposes, our worrying lapses, our grave errors, our overall worth. He gives us permission to bare our souls, to be candidly introspective, but not least, to smile at ourselves, to be grateful for the continuing opportunity we have to make recompense for our failures of omission or commission.

He extends to us, really, moments of a doctor's self-recognition—rendered in such a way that the particular becomes the universal, and the instantly recognizable: the function, the great advantage of all first-rate art. And not to be forgotten in this age of glib, overwrought formulations, of theories and more theories, of conceptualizations meant to explain (and explain away) anything and everything, he brings to us ironies, paradoxes, inconsistencies, contradictions—the small vignette which opens up a world of pleasurable, startling, or forbidden mystery. Doc Williams becomes William Carlos Williams the accomplished fabulist, anecdotist—and as well, the medical and social historian who takes the risks of autobiography. There were poems similarly harnessed, intended, and even journal entries, as in this wonderful statement found in the "little red notebook" Williams the Rutherford School Physician kept in 1914:

I bless the muscles
of their legs, their
necks that are

limber, their hair
that is like new
grass, their eyes
that are not
always dancing
their postures
so naive and
graceful, their
voices that are
full of fright &
other passions
their transparent
shams & their
mimicry of adults
—the softness of
their bodies—

As I read through, once more, these medical stories, these
medical poems, and the autobiographical account, "The
Practice," all so touching and blunt, both, I kept returning
to the words just quoted, to which I'd once heard him al-
lude, and which I remember him trying to remember, to
speak—the powerful, compelling, sensuousness of his mind,
with its offering of a hymn of love to those children, those
patients, those fellow human beings. On a few occasions
physicians invited him to come speak at their conferences,
their grand rounds, but he was shy, modest—afraid he had
little to say directly to his colleagues, no matter how much
he'd offered the world in general through his many and
varied writings. But he was dead wrong; he had everything
to say to us. He opens up the whole world, our world, to
us—and so, once again, as many in New Jersey had occasion
to say during the first half of this century, say and say
again: thank you, Doctor Williams.

Robert Coles, M.D.
March 1984
Cambridge, Massachusetts

THE DOCTOR STORIES

Mind and Body

FOR OURSELVES are we not each of us the center of the universe? It must be so, it is so for me, she said. It has always been so. I am the only one in my family who has had the courage to live for himself. Naturally, she added, we know that the rest of the world exists, but what has that to do with ourselves? Because someone says Sigrid Undset is a great writer, what of it? I don't think so. I will not read her books. To me they are dull. I am not a musician but writing must have some music in it to be readable and she has no music. I hate her. That is what I think and that is what I say.

I know people think I am a nut. I was an epileptic as a child. I know I am a manic depressive. But doctors are mostly fools. I have been very sick. They say it is my imagination. What is that? I know when I am sick and I have seen them. I saw a woman the same type as myself. The day before she died she was excited, as I am now, she would talk with you, argue as well as I am doing now. And the next day she was dead.

I have pains here, in my stomach. It has been terrible. For nine days I have been stopped. I feel it in my heart, like a cramp. It must be something. How can they say it is my imagination? They don't know. They're fools. Last night I got desperate and I cured myself with some soapy water. But I was worried. Can you blame me? So my husband says, Go on out and see an honest man. I have only ten dollars in my pocket, but I would pay fifty, if I had it, to find out. What is the matter with me?

1

They always get mad at me because I manage to find out what they are thinking. I got hold of the chart and I saw that it said "Neo-plasm." I knew from my Greek what that meant, new growth. That means a tumor. But I don't think the Doc himself knew when he read the report.

He examined me a dozen times and his theory was (I could overhear him talking to his assistant): I try this and then if it doesn't work I try that, then I try something else. When something works that is the way I find out what is the matter with the patient. I knew from his questions that he wanted to give me the filthiest diseases. He put everything on me. I could taste the carbolic in my mouth, and the mercury. I know that he painted me with silver nitrate because I heard the assistant say, "My God what has she been doing to herself?" But it was he who did it. I got sick of him finally and went home.

And what do you think he said to me? He said that what I needed was a man. What do you think of that? I told him I had a man at home, and a very good one. What do you think I have, a cancer? I bleed every once in a while. Tell me what you think. I don't care if I die. Nothing frightens me. But I am tired of dealing with fools.

I ventured to ask her if she had tried Atropin and Luminal for her colitis. They're no good for me, she said. Everything works the opposite from what it does in anyone else. I take Atropin for a few days then it dries my mouth, makes me worse than I was before. Luminal does not quiet me, it keeps me awake. No, there is nothing in that, nothing in that.

Tell me more of the history, I said. You have been operated on?

Yes, eighteen years ago, they took out the appendix, they said it was all tied up with the right ovary. A doctor had examined me and said there was something wrong on the left side. When I was opened up they found nothing there at all. Perhaps it is that, perhaps it is the adhesions, bands that pull sometimes. Anyhow it is not imagination.

I knew the story of her past. Her father had been a Norwegian sea captain, one of the better known of the old sailing families, powerful physique, a man who would be away for months, seldom at home. Her mother, also a Norse woman, had been frail, dying when Ingrid and her sister and two brothers were still children. On the father's side there had been several who had spent their last days in an asylum.

I am compensating for my childhood now, she continued. I do not believe in being repressed. I am the only one of my family that lets go. If I tire you, you must forgive me. When I have talked it out I feel better. I have to spit it out on someone. I do not believe in being good, in holding back. You're not too good, are you? People like that make me tired. Martyrs too, they're perverted, I detest them. I tell them they're the most selfish people on earth. Nobody wants them to be martyrs but themselves. They do it because it gives them pleasure. I say to them, all right, you are good. What does that mean? It means that goodness is its own reward. Don't expect to get paid for it. You have chosen that selfishly, just the same as I choose to do as I please. They are hypocrites if they want more. Everyone must choose for himself. Is it not so? I do not expect people to thank me if I do what I please.

She turned and said to my wife Emily who was sitting near her, your hair would look better if you took more care of it. You should do it. Look at my hair. Her hair was bobbed rather long and was of a reddish chestnut, a great flamelike mane which stood up almost flickeringly above her right ear. I think the hair can reflect the way we are. I can will my hair to be glossy and a better color. Of course you must brush it. But even if I am sick I can make it look well. I remember once I saw your mother, she turned again to Emily, and I saw she was not careful with herself, so I told her: You should take more care of your hair. You look like a servant girl.

People should speak out what is in their minds. Don't you think so? We should believe in ourselves. When I was confirmed in the Lutheran Church . . . How do you think I look?

Marvelous, I said, I never saw you looking better.

She laughed. It is because I do not worry. I am nervous, yes, but I do not worry. I simply want to know what is the matter with me. I have no inhibitions. That is why my face is smooth. In the hospital they were kidding me. They said, What is that girl doing here? They said I looked nineteen years old. And I do, sometimes.

It was true. I knew she was in her forties, but she looked clear-eyed, her complexion was ruddy, her skin smooth. Her bearing was alert, her movements perhaps too quick but not pathological.

People should speak out what is in their minds. Don't you think so? We should believe in ourselves. It took me a long time to learn that. It first came to me in college. My mother always wanted us to learn, to get up in the world.

She had won a scholarship from a Brooklyn high school to Cornell where she had majored in Latin, Greek and Logic, and again won a fellowship in Logic. The instructors retreated in disorder before her attacks till she quit the game and, needing money, went to teach Latin in a high school from which, after a month, she ran away. The slowness of the pupils drove her mad. From there she went to a New York business school, graduated in no time and became private secretary to one of New York's leading merchants—managing his affairs single handed when he was absent, a huge organization, a lieutenant in whom he had implicit confidence till he died.

What is book learning? she went on. Nothing at all. College ruins everything that is original in the young. It comes just in their formative years and if they have anything original in them by teaching them to copy, copy, copy, we ruin it all.

It may be true for some, I broke in, but to me it is the attitude which is taken toward it that counts. To me, what I intend for my boys, if they wish to go, is that it is a ticket. If they go in there, without reverence for the knowledge of their instructors but take it all just as a means for something which they need, I don't think it will hurt them.

Maybe you are right, she agreed, it is the attitude—if they can take it properly—which counts. But I ate it up out of books. Finally it turned me cold. Those men know nothing at all. It is life, what we see and decide for ourselves, that counts.

When I was confirmed in the Lutheran Church—to please my mother—when I was learning the catechism, I asked the preacher if I had to believe everything he said was true. And if I didn't believe it would I go to Hell? And if all the others in the other churches would go to Hell because they didn't believe it? For that was something that I didn't believe at all. All the others say the same thing to their people. How ridiculous that is? I told him.

He was shocked, she went on, and told me it was wicked for me to talk that way. So I perjured myself and joined the church to please my mother.

It is all fear. When we were children my mother would lie on the bed and pray to God to spare us from the lightning. I thought that was ridiculous. I said to her, How foolish. If God wants to strike me down, is it for me to ask him to spare me? I never felt afraid. If I am hit, what of it?

But Yates is afraid. Yates is her husband. He does not like lightning.

That's odd, I commented. For I knew him to be a steady Catholic.

Yes, he is afraid of it.

Did you not become a Catholic when you married him? asked Emily.

Yes, I did, said she. Why not? This is the way I felt. Yates was brought up by the Jesuits. His old father and mother are still in Ireland. He offered to join my church but I knew what that would mean. They might even say we were not married at all, and I knew how that would hurt his family.

Yates, she had met, incredibly, in an asylum where she had been confined after her breakdown. She had gone there of her own will to be cured and there she had decided to remain, to become a nurse to attend the insane. She thought that her life work at the time. And there she had encountered little, lame Yates, the gentle-voiced and kindly nurse —employed in the care of male patients, as she was in the care of females. It had been a most happy marriage, she with her erratic voluble disposition, he with his placid mind.

What should I do? she continued. I saw that he was not the kind to question himself intimately.

How is he? asked Emily who greatly admired the little Irishman. Why didn't you bring him out with you today?

Oh, I told him I didn't need him, said she. After last night when I thought I was going to die I felt so much better today that I told him I wanted to come alone. He's working and I didn't want to take him away from his work. What was I saying, oh yes, she continued, you remember what Caesar says in his Commentaries about the barbarians. It is better for them to have their barbaric worship than no religion at all. Let them cling to it.

Yes, what was the use of my asking him to give up his religion? He believes in his dogma and it is a comfort to him. He feels a part of it. That is what makes the Irish whole as a nation, their religion. They feel something solid under their feet and so they have courage to go ahead.

Like the Jews, I said.

Yes, exactly. It is their religion. So I said to myself, to keep that for him I won't ask him to join my church but I will join his. He has that and his nursing and it makes him happy. If I take that away what could I give him in return? He would be lost. When I was talking to the Jesuit, who came to teach me what the church meant, I told him I could not believe that. He said, I should. I asked him, Do you? But he did not answer me.

And I'm a little superstitious too, she went on. When I was in the hospital I stopped breathing. I said to myself, Why go on any more? Next time my breath stops I will not breathe again and then it will be done. I didn't care. They asked me where I wanted to be sent. At first I didn't know what they meant. Then I caught it. They meant after I was dead. So I gave them all the details.

But Yates got nervous, so without telling me anything about it he had the priest come up to me to give me the sacrament. I was surprised but, I tell you something came over me and I felt happy. I felt that I wanted to live. I do not believe all the stuff they tell you. But I must say that I was glad.

Yes, I agree with you, it is a comfort, no doubt. But what about Socrates? He took the cup quietly—without religion.

Oh, you have read that too, she said and seemed pleased.

Yes, I went on. It is good to feel a solidarity with a group but do not forget that that kindly old priest by telling you that there is just one way to be saved, by excluding all the other people of the earth represents a cruelty of the most inhuman sort. For myself, I went on, if I were dying in Africa and the chief of the tribe who was my friend asked the chief medicine man to do a ceremonial dance for me, with beating of tom toms to conduct me into the other world, I should feel a real comfort which I believe would be a greater solace to me than the formula of some kindly priest.

I suppose so, she added, but it is the same: Someone to tell our troubles to is what we need. I suppose I bore you with all I am saying today but I must talk. You must think

I'm crazy. When I go away for two or three days Nuffie
stays in my chair till I come back.

What is that? I said.

She laughed. Nuffie is my little dog. It is a Spaniel. She
stays in my chair till I come home. Would you believe it,
when I have bronchitis or anything she will come up to me
and smell around my chest until she finds the place where
I have a pain. Then she will lick that place and the pain goes
right away.

I laughed.

You don't believe it, but it is true.

You mean she can smell a pain?

Well, I don't know. Dogs have a special sense. I think
they know more than we do at times. Anyhow it is so.
Perhaps she hears the little râles, with her sharp ears. You
do not believe me, do you?

How can I doubt you? I said.

I believe in such things as second sight, said she. Sometimes I quarrel with my sister. And the dog does not like
that. She goes away. We both have hard heads. We take
opposite sides and neither one wants to give in. But this
time Nuffie went to my sister and consoled her first. I was
furious. So I stopped talking. I thought if Nuffie did that
she was right. And then she came over to console me. But
she went to my sister first. I said no more.

Yes, I believe in second sight. You know how I am. I
say what is in my mind and people don't like that. So I had
a quarrel with my brother-in-law. We didn't speak to each
other for a year. Then one day I saw a tall fellow carrying
two cans of paint on the street and I knew it was he. I
went past him and we did not say anything to each other.
But when I got past I turned around and so did he. We each
did that three times. But we did not speak. It scared me. I
said to myself, he is going to die and he is calling me to go
with him. Would you believe that?

He was perfectly well, mind you, but that is what I

thought. Then within a month he caught pneumonia and he sent for me. I was so glad to have a chance to talk to him and to comfort him. I saw at once that he was a dead man but my sister could not see it. She cannot see those things in people's faces. She thought he was going to get well. He asked me what I thought about it, and I could see that it exhausted him even to talk that much. But I said of course he would recover; to rest and it would be all right. I had to say that and I could see that he was easier. But he died next day. I was frightened then, perhaps that is what is the matter with me now. My parents died at forty-five and fifty-two. Add them together and divide by two and you will get the age at which you yourself will die. That is this year. Don't you think you'd better go upstairs and get your clothes off if you want me to examine you? I asked her.

Yes, she said, it's getting late. I know I'm an awful nuisance. Where shall I go? In the office? Upstairs. All right. You won't see anything much, she added, with a wry face. I am nothing at all now. Just like a man. My legs are hairy like my husband's. I have often wondered what sex I am, she laughed. I used to wonder as a child with my flat chest and my narrow hips if I was not more a man than a woman. I am sure I am more a man than Yates is, she commented.

Yes, I put in, aren't we all more or less that way—fortunately.

Certainly it is so.

Perhaps your trouble is that you need some woman to love.

I have always loved women more than men, she agreed. Always. It amuses me. In the hospital the nurses used to kid me. They used to say, Look out for her, she's that way. I enjoyed it.

When she was lying on the bed half-bared she spoke again of her physique:

I have no lung trouble, of that I am sure for I have a

good chest like my father. But I have nothing else to show you to thrill you. When I was being examined the old fool of a doctor—it is always an old man who thinks you are trying to flirt with him—the young ones know better. The old fool tried to tickle me. I felt nothing at all. I asked him what he was trying to do, so he stopped.

I carefully palpated her abdomen but could find nothing at all. Truly she was built like a man, narrow hips, broad deep chest and barely any breasts to speak of. Her heart action was even and regular. Only flushed cheeks, the suggestively maniacal eyes, the quiver of the small muscles of the face, her trembling fingers told her stress. She awaited my verdict with silence at last. I could find nothing.

Yes, she said, only two men have found the exact spot. And she pointed to a place in her right iliac quadrant. One was a young doctor at the Post Graduate Hospital who has become famous since then, and another was the surgeon who operated on me the first time. The rest just feel around the abdomen as you have done.

But do not forget, I said in my own defense, that there is a place in the abdomen in major hysteria which if it is pressed upon will definitely bring on a convulsive attack.

She looked at me with interest.

Yes, the Greeks connected it with those organs. That is its name. Perhaps I should have everything cut out.

Not on your life, I told her.

No, I believe that too. I don't want any more operations. So you do not think I have a cancer.

Not from the evidence I have found so far. If I could see the X-rays I might have a different opinion, but I do not think so. From what you say and the length of time that the symptoms have been going on, the fact that you have not lost weight, that you are ruddy and well—I believe that you are suffering merely—but that is quite enough—from what Llwelyn C. Barker calls—I have forgotten the term—what we used to call mucous colitis. It is a spasm of the large intestine which simulates all sorts of illnesses for which people are frequently operated on.

I left the room while she dressed. While I was away she told my wife: I want to live because I have found my place in life. I am a housekeeper. I have my husband and my work to do and that is my world. I have found, she added, that we must live for others, that we are not alone in the world and we cannot live alone.

To me she said when I had taken her to the bus and we were waiting: Well, you haven't told me what is the matter with me. What is it? Don't tell me I am nervous.

There has never been an anatomic basis discovered for an opinion in cases like yours, I said, until recently. Apparently the cause was laid down in the germ plasm when you were created.

Yes, my family history is bad, she agreed. They were an old family, run down. Yes, I come from an old family. I should have married a robust type. But my inferiority complex would not let me. I did not take up when I had the chance. I didn't have the nerve. Instead I looked for someone that I could mother, someone to take care of. That is how I took to Yates, he needed me so much. I wonder what was the matter with him. He didn't walk till he was twelve with his big head and little legs.

The anatomic basis for your condition, I continued, seems to have been detected in a new study called capillaroscopy, a study of the microscopic terminal blood vessels. In people of your type these terminal loops between the arteries and the veins are long and gracile. They are frail, expand and contract easily, it is the cause of all the unstable nervous phenomena which you see.

Yes, I can feel it often, she agreed. The blood goes into my face or into my brain. I often want to run or scream out, it is so hard for me to stand it.

Others have short more or less inert loops. Those are the lethargic types, the stable, even dispositions.

Here's the bus, she cried out. Good-bye. And she grasped the tips of my fingers in her hurry to be gone.

Good-bye, I called after her. Bring Yates with you next time. Remember me to him. Good-bye, good-bye.

Old Doc Rivers

Horses. These definitely should be taken into consideration in estimating Rivers position, along with the bad roads, the difficult means of communication of those times.

For a physician everything depended on horses. They were a factor determining his life.

Rivers prided himself on his teams. It was something to look at when he came down the street in the rubber-tired sulky with the red wheels. He'd sit there peering out under the brim of his hat with that smile of his always on his face, confident, a little disdainful, but not unfriendly.

He knew them all. . . .

Hello, Frank, how's the wife? .

Not so good, Doc.

The old trouble, eh? Tell you what I'll do. I'll drive around and take ner up to the hospital this afternoon.

Can't get her to do it, Doc.

Scared?

Guess you hit it.

All right, you old rascal; have a cigar. And he'd turn away, with the horses pawing and shaking their heads right and left, ready to go.

A young man and a bachelor, this was the happiest period of his life, when he was exhilarated by an occupation, the sun, the cold, the motion of the horses, their haunches working muscularly before him as he sat and smoked. Maybe it was that and a mad rush to get from place to place; it came and went in a moment. He saw it, realized it, there was nothing else and—he had the rest of his life to live.

This is how he practiced. . . .

Come in, Jerry—making a pass at him with his open hand
—How's the old soak?

Fer Christ's sake, Doc, lay off me. I'm sick.

Who's sick? Have a drap of the auld Crater. He nearly
always had a jug of it just behind his desk. Did a dog bite
you?

Look a' this damned neck of mine. Jesus, what the hell's
the matter with you? Easy, I says.

Shut up! You white-livered Hibernian.

Aw, Doc, fer Christ's sake, gimme a break.

What's the matter, did I do anything to you?

Listen, Doc, ain't ya gonna put something on it?

On what? Keep those pants buttoned. Sit down. Grab
onto these arms. And don't let go until I'm through or I'm
likely to slit you in half.

Yeow! Jesus, Mary and Joseph! Whadje do to me, Doc?

I think your throat's cut, Jerry. Here, drink this. Go lie
down over there a minute. I didn't think you were so
yellow.

What! Lie down? What for? Whadda you think I am,
a woman? Wow! Have you got any more of that liquor?
Say, you're some man, Doc. You're some man. What do
you get?

That's all right, Jerry, bring it around next week.

That's some relief.

The phone rang. It was one of the first in the region.
Wanted at the hospital.

Hey, Maggie!—to the dour old Irish woman who sullenly
cared for his world: Tell John to drive around to the side
door.

Wait a minute now, wait a minute. There's a woman out
there has been wantin' to see you for three days. She looks
real sick. She's been here all morning waitin' for you.

Get her in.

Doctor . . .

Yes, I know—he could see that her color was bad. Where is it? In your belly?

Yes, Doctor.

He made a quick examination, slipping on a rubber glove without removing his coat, washing his hands after at the basin in the corner of the room. The whole thing hadn't taken six minutes.

Leaning over his desk he scribbled two notes.

Take thirty drops of it tonight, in a little water. And here, here's a note to Sister Rose. Get up to the hospital in the morning. Don't eat any breakfast.

But, Doctor, what's the matter with me?

Now, now. Tomorrow morning. Don't worry, Mother. It'll be all right. Good-bye, and he pushed her out of the door.

John's waiting for you, said big Margaret as he was struggling with his coat, his hat, a cigar, stopping in the corner of the porch to light it. A few moments later he was into the carriage and off.

He leaned back, seeing nothing. The horses trotted up the Plank Road. Past the railroad cut. It was a dark spring night. The cherry blossoms were out on the McGee property. Past the nurseries. Down the steep hill by the swamp. The turn. By the Cadmus farm. The County Bridge; clattering over the boards. Over the creek. The creek was flowing swiftly, an outgoing tide, a few lights streaking it, a few sounds rising, a faint ripple and a cool air.

Naturally, he must have given value for value, good services for money received. He had a record of thirty years behind him, finally, for getting there (provided you could find him) anywhere, anytime, for anybody—no distinctions; and for doing something, mostly the right thing, without delay and of his own initiative, once he was there.

He was ready, energetic and courageous. The people were convinced that he knew his stuff—if anyone knew it.

And they would pay him well for his services—if they paid him at all.

But what could he do? What did he do? What kind of a doctor was he, really?

Thinking it over, it occurred to me to drop in at the hospital in the small nearby city where he took many of his operative cases to see for myself exactly what he had been about all these years. To satisfy myself, then, as to the man's scope I went to the St. Michael's Hospital of which I am speaking and induced the librarian to get out the older record books for me to look at.

As usual in such cases, something other than the thing desired first catches the eye.

These were heavy ledgers, serious and interesting in appearance with their worn leather covers and gold lettering across the front: Registry of Cases treated at St. Michael's Hospital, etc., etc. There were a dozen of them in all from the year 1898 on. I felt a catch at the throat before the summary of so much human misery.

Opening at random, there it lay, the whole story of the hospital, what had been done and the result, along with the doctors' names and other like information, listed in tall columns. These were carefully written in through the months and years in longhand of many characters, minute and tall, precise and free, in blue, in green, black, purple and even red; with stub pens, sharp pens and even pencil, across two full pages with two narrower fly leaves between.

I chose the years 1905 and 1908 and began to thumb over the leaves looking for Rivers' name. But my eye fell instead upon the list of patients' occupations. Such a short time ago and yet some of these entries struck me as odd: Liveryman, coachman, bartender! Nothing in years has so impressed me with the swiftness of time's flight.

In the doctors' column, there was Rivers, dead surely of the effects of his addiction, but here another who had shot himself in despair at the outcome, it is said, of an affair with the wife of another physician on the same page, his friend. While this one had divorced his wife and married once again—a younger woman. Another at sixty had quietly laid himself down upon his office couch and said good-bye and died. This one had left town hurriedly taking himself to the coast, possibly to escape jail—leaving a wife and child behind him. Some had grown old in the profession and been forgotten though they were still alive. One of these, ninety and more, totally deaf, still morosely wandered the streets and scarcely anyone remembered that he had been a doctor. Queer, all that since 1908.

What had Rivers really accomplished?

Surgically, there were, to be sure, more than enough of the usual scrapings, and appendicitis was common. But here is a list of some of his undertakings; I copy from the records: endometritis, salpingitis, contracture of the hand, ruptured spleen, hernia, lacerations (some accident, no doubt). There were malignancies of the bowel, excisions of the thyroid, breast amputations; here an ununited fracture of the humerus involving the insertion of a plate and marked "Cured" in the final column. There were normal maternity cases, Caesarean sections, ruptured ectopic pregnancies. He treated fistulas, empyema, hydrocele. He performed hysterectomies, gastro-enterostomies, gall bladder resections. He even tackled a deviated nasal septum. There were fractures of all the bones of the body, nearly, and many of those of the head, simple and compound.

And at the far edge of the right-hand page, you would see the brief legend "Cured" as often following his name as that of any other doctor.

On the medical side, the old familiar "neurasthenia" which meant that they never did discover what was the matter with the patient; but also nephritis, pneumonia, endocarditis, rheumatism, malaria and typhoid fever. Most left the hospital cured.

And who were they? Plumber, nurseryman, farmer,

saloonkeeper (with hob-nail liver), painter, printer, house-wife, that's the way it would go. It was a long and interest-ing list of the occupations of the region from tea merchant to no occupation at all.

Acute alcoholism and D.T. were frequent entries.

It was not money. It came of his sensitivity, his civility; it was that that made him do it, I'm sure; the antithesis rather of that hog-like complacency that comes to so many men following the successful scamper for cash. Nervous, he accepted his life at its own terms and never let it beat him—to no matter what extremity he was driven.

But sometimes I know he had to quit an operation half way through and have another finish it for him. Or perhaps he would retire for a moment (we all knew why), return, change his gloves, and continue. The transformation in him would be striking. From a haggard old man he would be changed "like that" into a resourceful and alert operator.

Going further, I asked several men who had been in the habit of standing opposite him across the operating table their opinion of him as a surgeon—what had been the secret of his success.

Again, I began to pick up odd pieces of news. Dr. Jami-son, who had been an intern in the hospital during several of Rivers' most active years, recalled how he would awaken sometimes in his room on the first floor at night to find Rivers asleep outside the covers on his bed beside him snor-ing like a good fellow. And once on a trip to the state hospital for mental diseases at Nashawan, one of the attend-ants of the place had come up to the group to ask them if the person he had found in a semi-conscious condition leaning against the wall down the corridor was one of their party. It was Rivers; something had gone wrong with his usual arrangements and he was coked to the eyes.

In sum, his ability lay first in an uncanny sense for diagnosis. Then, he didn't flounder. He made up his mind and went to it. Furthermore, he was not, as might be supposed, radical and eccentric in his surgical technique but conservative and thoroughgoing throughout. He was not nervous but cool and painstaking—so long as he had the drug in him. His principles were sound, nor was he exhibitionistic in any sense of the word.

And what a psychologist he was. There was a boy down in Kingsland who had had diarrhoea for about a week. Several doctors had seen him and prescribed medicine but the child had been eating almost anything he wanted. Finally they called in Rivers. He pulled down the kid's pants, took one look and said, Hell, what he needs is a circumcision. And he did it, there and then, kept food away from him a day or two (because of the operation) and of course the kid got well. That's how smart he was.

Only twice did I personally assist him at operations.

The first case was that of a man called Milliken, an enormous, hulking fellow in his late thirties, swarthy, hairy-chested and with arms and legs on him fit for the strong man in the circus. He ran a milk route at one end of the town. It was acute appendicitis.

When we got to the little house where he lived, a double house I recall, the only room big enough to handle him in was the parlor. We rigged up a table in the usual way. Rivers said we were ready and told the big boy to climb on up. Which he did.

I forgot to mention that Milliken was a great drinker. He also forgot to mention it to me at the time.

Go ahead with the ether, said Rivers.

Well, it didn't take me long—not more than twenty minutes—to find out that ether wouldn't touch this fellow anyway you gave it—unless it might be by a tube. There are individuals like that, powerfully muscled men and alcoholics.

By this time Rivers and his assistant were ready

Wait a minute, Doc, managed to mumble the patient.

For, strange to say, the man had been docile up to that point so that we thought he was under. But it was not so.

I could see that Rivers was losing patience but I was already pouring a stream of ether upon the mask. They were ready for the incision, scrubbed up, the sheet in place, just waiting.

Rivers was fidgeting and I wasn't in a particularly pleasant mood myself. Finally he spoke sharply to me asking if I didn't know how to give an anesthetic. I could feel my face flush but I didn't say anything. Instead I took out the chloroform and began to give that, carefully. Rivers looked approval but said nothing. We all waited a moment or two for this to take effect. By this time, we were all sweating and mad—at the patient, each other, and ourselves.

The outcome was that, after three attempts at an incision —at which time an earthquake occurred under our grips, Rivers gave it up and turned to me.

Here, he said, Gimme that mask. Come up here and assist Willie. I'll show you how to get this man under.

I wanted to scrub. He said, No, put on the gloves. I obeyed. There was nothing else to do. Asepsis had gone to the winds long since in our efforts to keep the man from walking out of the room.

Rivers just took the chloroform bottle and poured the stuff into that Bohunk. I expected to see him turn black and pass out.

But he didn't.

After a few minutes, we were told by Rivers to go ahead.

His assistant just touched the skin with his knife and up flew the man's knees. I was tickled to death.

Go ahead, go ahead, cried Rivers excitedly, hold him down and go to it.

That's what we did. One man held the head and arms. I finally quit entirely as an assistant, lay on my stomach across the man's thighs and grasped the legs of the table on the other side. One man, alone, did the actual work. It is to his credit that he did it well.

It must have been a month after that I saw the patient, one day, standing in front of the fire house. Curious, I went up to him to find out if he had felt anything while the operation had been going on.

At first he didn't know me, but when I told him who I was, expecting to get a crack in the eye maybe for my trouble, he came up with a start:

Did I feel anything? said he. My God, every bit of it, every bit of it. But he was a well man by that time.

It was the case though of an old German harness maker of East Hazleton, Frankel by name, which first raised doubts in my mind as to Rivers' actual condition. I received the call one day and went to the address given, where I knew the old man and his wife lived above the store.

They had the kitchen already rigged up as an operating room, a plain deal table with a smaller one at the foot of it with blankets and a sheet over them for the old man to lie on. There were sterile dressings, the instruments were boiling on the gas stove and everything was in good order as far as I could make out.

As soon as I had entered, Rivers called into the hall for the old fellow to come on along, we were ready for him. He had been in bed in the front of the house and I shall never forget my surprise and the shock to my sense of propriety when I saw Frankel, whom I knew, coming down the narrow, dark corridor of the apartment in his bare feet and an old-fashioned nightgown that reached just to his knees. He was holding his painful belly with both hands while his scared wife accompanied him solicitously on one side.

The old fellow was too sick for that sort of thing but Rivers just motioned him without a word uttered to climb up on the table where they put another sheet over him and

I was told to start the anesthetic. I did so, silent, and not too well pleased with the way things were going.

Rivers asked the wife if she had any more of that good whisky about the place. She brought it out. He poured himself nearly a tumblerful, filled the glass with water at the sink and, while he was drinking, held up the flask with the other hand toward his confrere and to me, gesturing. We refused. With that he finished his glass, plugged the cork in the bottle and dropped it into the side pocket of his coat which hung nearby on a chair.

He was in his undershirt and suspenders, sleeves rolled up. From this time forward, things went ahead normally and properly, more or less, according to the usual operating-room technique of the time.

Rivers made the incision. He took one look and shrugged his shoulders. It was a ruptured appendix with advanced general peritonitis. He shoved in a drain and let it go at that, the right thing to do. But the patient died next day.

I tell you there was a howl about the town: another decent citizen done to death by that dope fiend Rivers. Several of my friends cautioned me to watch my step. You may be sure, in any case, that I thought carefully over what had occurred but I did not come to any immediate conclusion.

And yet the man could be—often was—kindly, alert, courteous. Most interesting it is to hear that he played the violin excellently and would often spend an evening, in the early days, playing duets with the one musician of any note that could be encountered in the neighborhood—the organist at the nearby cathedral.

When little Virginia Shippen, aged five, had a kidney complication following scarlet fever, Rivers came in day and night, did—as he thought—everything that could be done to save her. Still she remained unconscious, dropsical; the kidneys had ceased to function. One evening Rivers told them that he was through—that she would be dead by morning.

At this point, the mother asked if he would object if she made a suggestion. She wanted to try flaxseed poultices over the kidney regions. Go ahead, said Rivers.

The next day the child's kidneys had started slowly to function, sanguineous, muddy stuff, but she was conscious and her fever had dropped. Rivers was delighted, praised the mother and told her that she had taught him something. The child grew up and lived thirty years thereafter.

He was short with women:

Well, Mary, what is it?

I have a pain in my side, doctor.

How long have you had it, Mary?

Today, doctor. It's the first time.

Just today.

Yes, doctor.

Climb up on the table. Pull up your dress. Throw that sheet over you. Come on, come on. Up with you. Come on now, Mary. Pull up your knees.

Ooh!

He could be cruel and crude. And like all who are so, he could be sentimentally tender also, and painstaking without measure.

A young woman, one of my early friends and patients, spoke to me of his kindness to her. Her foster parents—for she was an adopted child—would never have anyone else. For months she went to him, two and three times a week, while he with the greatest gentleness and patience treated her. It was a nasopharyngeal condition of some sort, difficult to manage. Little by little, he brought her along till she was well, charging them next to nothing for his services.

Money was never an end with him.

The end was, he made this girl, who was frail and gentle, one of his lifelong admirers.

But on another occasion in the drug store one day a boy

about ten came up to him with a sizable abscess on his neck. They had not been able to find the doctor in his office so the boy had followed him there.

Come here, said Rivers, Let's see. And with that he took a scalpel out of his vest pocket, and made a swipe at the thing.

But the boy was too quick. He jerked back and the knife caught him low. He turned and ran, bleeding and yelling, out of the door. Rivers chuckled and paid no further attention to the incident.

Naturally there were certain favorite places which he'd visit more often than others. First of all was the Jeannette Mansion in Crestboro, two miles above Hazleton north along the ridge, where a number of French families had settled sixty or eighty years previously.

They were rather a different class, these Fench, from some of the other inhabitants of the region and showed it by keeping a great deal to themselves in their large manor houses surrounded by the billowy luxuriance of tall trees.

A fence, the beginning of all culture, invariably surrounded the property as a frame, giving a sense of propriety and measure. Ease and retirement seemed to blossom here, though naturally this was often an appearance only.

Not, I think, that these things meant anything consciously to Rivers, but they were there and he passed among them. In that way they must have influenced him more than a little. For he liked it all, obviously. Though, of course, it was the people really who attracted him.

He was a Frenchman, an Alsatian—I can't think of his name, said my informer, old Dr. Trowbridge. When you get older, your memory is not so good. Wait a minute. No, well, anyway, he went back to France. So and so lives in the house now. He had several daughters—they were a very gay family.

I had been asking the old doctor how it was that Rivers began to take the dope. Oh, he must have been taking

something before he came here. I don't know how else to
explain his eccentricity. Anyway, when he went to Europe,
to Freiburg to study with Seibert, the pathologist (I don't
think he studied very much), this man, oh, what is his name?
he had gone back to France—had to give Rivers the money
to return to America.

Jeannette, that's it—he was a high liver. He built himself
a greenhouse in the back and put all kinds of plants in it.
He must have spent hundreds and hundreds of dollars on
it. He would sit out there and play cards with his friends.
Not difficult surely to understand the attraction this had
for the tormented doctor. For, if Jeannette was a volup-
tuary, his friend Rivers was no laggard before any lead
which he could find it in his conscience to propose.

To play cards, to laugh, talk and partake with the Frenchman of his imported wines and liquors was good. After a
snowstorm, of a Sunday morning, to sit there at ease—out
of reach of patients—in a tropical environment and talk,
sip wines and enjoy a good cigar—that was something. It
was a quaint situation, too, in that crude environment of
those days, so altogether foreign, incongruous and delight-
fully aloof.

It would take a continental understanding—reinforced
as it is by centuries of culture—to comprehend and to
accept the complexities and contradictions of a nature such
as Rivers'. Not in the provincial bottom of the New Jersey
of that time had the doctor found such another release.

The man was now at the height of his popularity and
power.

Intelligence he had and force—but he also had nerves,
a refinement of the sensibilities that made him, though able,
the victim of the very things he best served. This was the
man himself whom the drug retrieved.

He was far and away by natural endowment the ablest individual of our environment, a serious indictment against all
the evangelism of American life which I most hated—at the

same time a man trying to fill his place among those lacking the power to grasp his innate capabilities.

I don't believe Jeannette doped. It cannot have been other than as to a last hope, a veritable island of safety, that Rivers went to the mansion. The only influence that might possibly have saved him, as they say, had it but been known. In any case, they were gay and the time passed; at the mansion he was free, enlivened—then when that was finished, he was again beaten.

The mansion was relaxation to him, but he couldn't live there and his restlessness would in the end pass beyond it.

No doubt, there would be periods when he didn't hit the dope for months at a time. Then he'd get taking it again. Finally he'd feel himself slipping and he'd head off— overnight sometimes—leaving his practice as it might lie— for the woods.

This flight to the woods or something like it, is a thing we most of us have yearned for at one time or another, particularly those of us who live in the big cities. As Rivers did. For in their jumble we have lost touch with ourselves, have become indeed not authentic persons, but fantastic shapes in some gigantic fever dream. He, at least, had the courage to break with it and to go.

With this pressure upon us, we eventually do what all herded things do; we begin to hurry to escape it, then we break into a trot, finally into a mad run (watches in our hands), having no idea where we are going and having no time to find out.

He wanted to plunge into something bigger than himself. Primitive, physically sapping. Maine gave it. To hunt the deer. He'd bring them home and give cuts of venison around to all his friends.

But that, too, ended pretty badly. After his eyes had been affected, by abuse and illness, he one day by accident shot his best friend in the woods, a guide he always followed, shot him through the temples as dead as a door nail.

Characteristic of the man is it that he made amends to the unfortunate's family faithfully as best he could, everything that was asked of him, to the last penny. And then, when the last payment had been made, he invited a young doctor of his acquaintance to dinner with him in New York —for a rousing celebration.

Rivers made a hobby one time of catching rattlesnakes, which abound in the mountains of North Jersey. He enjoyed the sport and the danger, apparently, while there was a scientific twist to it in that the venom they collected was to be used for laboratory work in New York.

A patient of mine gave me an impression of his office as it looked in those days:

There were six of us kids, brothers and sisters. I myself must have been about ten years old. We used to go up and sit there Sunday mornings. We'd be crazy for it. We used to like to look at his trophies. He had 'em too, moose and deer heads up on the wall and fish of all kinds.

He was a great hunter. I remember one time he was telling my father how he was bitten by a rattler, on the arm. Being a doctor, he knew what he was up against. He asked his guide to take his knife and cut the place out. But the guide didn't have the nerve. So the Doc took his own hunting knife in the other hand and sliced it wide open and sucked the blood out of it. I suppose he took a shot of dope first to steady himself. We were in the office with my father and he rolled up his sleeve and showed us the cut—right down the middle of his arm.

It was about this time too that he once had Charlie Hensel in to see him, one evening when there were quite a few others besides, out in the waiting room. Put on the gloves, Charlie, he said—he always had a couple of pairs of them lying around the place somewhere—and let's see what you can do.

But Charlie was good in those days and he knew the Doc

was in no shape for him to be roughing it up with. He shook his head and said, No, not tonight, Doc.

That nettled Rivers. Scared? he said. What's the matter, a young fella like you? Come on, put'em on.

All right, said Charlie in his sweet, easy voice. Just as you say. He told me the story shortly after it happened.

So they started in to spar after pushing back the desk and clearing a little space for themselves.

Charlie tapped the old boy lightly on the face a couple of times keeping away from the body. At this the Doc let go a hot one for Charlie's middle.

Come on, come on, he kept saying.

But Charlie could see that the Doc was getting winded so he tapped him again and was going to say he guessed that would be enough for tonight when the Doc drove in a swift one which caught Charlie on the temple just as he was going to drop his hands. Come on, come on, he said once more, a young fella like you.

So Charlie, wanting to end the business, feinted, just easy and then lifted the Doc one under the chin that sent him staggering backward to the wall. There he sat down unexpectedly in the consultation chair they had placed back out of the way. It shook the building.

The trouble with you, Charlie—the trouble with hitting you, Charlie, said the Doc slowly after a while, is that you ain't got any belly at all. Which was true enough. Charlie was very narrow across the middle then—like a sailor.

He'd have spells when his brother even could do nothing with him. He would go completely mad. He put in several sessions at the State Insane Asylum—six months or more—on at least two occasions.

When he'd been there a month or so, he'd begin to ask the Superintendent, who was a friend of his, whether he didn't think he could go out to work again. You're as good a doctor as I am, old man, would say this one finally. If you think you can make it, go ahead. And back he'd turn again to the old grind.

Then one winter he got so low with typhoid fever that it looked as if this time the game was up. They wanted a nurse; he refused to have one. And nobody wanted him as a patient either. He was completely gone with dope and the disease. Finally he himself asked for a girl he had known some years before at Blockley Hospital, a nurse he had once seen there and admired.

She took on the case.

He married her when he was able to be up and about again, and they went to Europe on a honeymoon. No doubt, she loved him.

Yes, I can remember his wife, said a lady to me. When she first came out she was a pretty little thing, just like anybody else. But I can still see her one day when she came into the store knocking against the counters, first on one side then on the other; she was covered with diamonds, her hands and her neck—she didn't seem to know where she was going. Her face didn't seem to be bigger than the palm of my hand.

A great many of his more respectable friends left him now. They'd still call him—if he was right—but he was too greatly distrusted.

You know how it used to be, said one of my best friends to me one day much to my surprise. You'd get some doctor and fool around with him for a while and get another and they'd all say something different and you wouldn't know where the hell you were. And this is the story he told me:

Well, this happened many years ago. I was sick and my old man was worried. Finally the druggist tipped us off. Get Rivers, he said. He's a dope but when he's right you can't beat him. And I tell you what I'll do—because he knew the old man well and he himself had been something of a rounder in his day—I'll call up Rivers and get him down here at the store. And, if he's right, I'll send him up.

So he did.

Later in the day when the Doc came into the room he took one look at me. This boy's got typhoid fever, he said. Just like that—that's how he did it. And I'll tell you what I'll do. To prove it, I'll take his blood now and send it in to my brother—he was doing nothing but blood work at that time—and I'll let you know in a few days.

Sure enough, he was right. He had the jump on the thing. The result was I had a light case and we had Rivers for years after that as our family physician.

He'd sit at the table writing a prescription and you could see his head fall down lower and lower—he'd go to sleep right there, right in front of your eyes. My old man would shake him every once in a while and finally he'd get up and go out.

When he started to hit the dope, his brother did his best to get him into some hospital in the city. He knew he was good and, if he could get him in there in a proper atmosphere, he thought he could save him. But the old boy was too foxy. He liked it out here, his friends, the life or whatever it was and they couldn't move him.

The thing, one of the main things, that got the other doctors down on him was his habit of going off—just disappearing sometimes. He liked to go fishing, and he was a crack shot. He'd have important cases, or anything. But that didn't make any difference. You'd call him up to find out why he hadn't been there and they'd say, He's gone away for a few days, we don't know where.

All you could do was get another doctor.

A couple of years after that, one summer when my old man had gone off on a trip somewhere, he sent me down to the only boarding house in town—you know where I mean. He'd left me in the house alone the year before and he wasn't any too satisfied with some of the things we pulled off while he was away. Well, this time Rivers heard of it and wanted me to come over and live with him.

I don't know how he got me out of there, but he did. The old gal who ran the place didn't want to let me go, knowing my father and all that. But Rivers persuaded her that I was sick, I guess, and needed treatment and that the best way for me was to live at his house where he could keep his eye on me. So I got my things together in two minutes, you can bet, and into his buggy I hopped and over we went.

My old man hasn't forgiven him for that to this day.

Sunday mornings were the times. It was a regular show. Because most of his patients were poor people and they could come only on Sunday. I'm telling you you never saw an office like it. He had the right idea, he was for humanity —put it any way you like. They'd be sitting all over the place, out in the hall, up the stairs, on the porch, anywhere they could park themselves.

When it was somebody that didn't know me, he'd say I was a young doctor. I was just seventeen then. He'd give me a white coat and tell me to come on. Jesus! Naturally I thought he was great. And I'll tell you in all those four months I never used to see any of those butcheries they'd talk about. Everything he did was O.K. I suppose I'd think different now, but then I thought he was a wonder.

I do remember one woman, though. God, it was a crime. You can imagine what I mean. Here I was, a kid never knowing anything at all. I was having the time of my life. Yes, everything, you're right. I held her while he did the job. I often think of it.

That was the romantic period of my life, those four months I lived with him.

He never kept any track of money. There wasn't a book around the place. Any money he got he shoved it in his pocket. But he never paid for anything, either.

Clever? That boy was there! He'd go over to his desk

and you'd see him fumbling around with some instruments. And right in front of you he'd give himself a shot and, unless you were wise, you wouldn't see him do it.

He was foxy too. He'd stall for a few minutes to give it time to act. That was when he had anything important to do. He'd wait a few minutes, then he'd come out steely-eyed and as quiet and steady as the best of them.

That was the difference between him and her. It made her crazy. She didn't know how to control it, but it steadied him down.

Many's the time he'd wake me up in the middle of the night to go out with him. Down at Johnny Kessler's was one of his hangouts where he'd go for soft-shell crabs and clam chowder.

Once he gave me some tickets for a show in New York. Some dirty racket, I've forgotten. He told me to get some of my friends and go in and have a good time. He gave us the tickets and started us off on his own liquor. It was the first show of that kind I'd ever taken in.

When I came home next morning, he himself took care of me, undressed me and put me to bed.

I can remember one night while I was living there, he waked me up at two o'clock in the morning. It was in summer, one of those hot, muggy nights. I'd been operated on too, the day before, he'd taken out my tonsils or something and I was feeling rotten. But that didn't make any difference, I had to go out with him just the same.

We got the old buggy and started out. We went down in the meadows, at two A.M. mind you, down to Mooney's saloon, the old halfway house, you know where it is. He went in and left me there. The mosquitos nearly ate me alive. He had a case in there or something, maybe he took a few drinks. I don't know what.

Anyway, I sat there slapping mosquitos. The old man came out after a while and told me the Doc was asleep and that they didn't want to wake him. So I, kid like, not wanting to make a fuss or anything, I said all right and just sat there. He left me there in that buggy till five A.M. Jesus!

Then he came out and we went home. When we got there, he said, Let's have some lamb chops! So out we went again, to the butcher's. He went to the door and of course it was closed. So he went up on the porch around at the side and stamped and banged until that fellow had to get up and come down and get him his chops out of the ice box.

Then we went home and he cooked them in the kitchen. And, say, he could cook. He was a wonderful cook. He could make a piece of meat taste like nothing in the world.

We ate the chops and then I went to bed.

When Doc wasn't in his office, he wasn't home, that's all.

When practice was light in summer and there'd be nothing else to do, as it happens sometimes to us all, he'd call his coachman and say, Hitch 'em up, Johnny—or Jake, or whoever it might be that was driving for him at the time—and start out, nobody at first knew whither.

Where are we headin', Doc?

He nodded to the left, down the hill.

It was a clear June day—the kids were still in school—about two in the afternoon. John let the horses jog lazily down the macadam.

Someone hailed him: Well, Doc, where you sneakin' off to? Swimmin'? The Doc gave the man a broad wink as much as to say: Go to hell.

Down near the track there was a bunch of willows by the ice house where the road turns before straightening out to go through the cat-tails. Maybe he saw them, maybe he didn't, you never knew.

Hello, Doc. Where ye goin'?

He just nodded his head. They just smiled and nodded in reply.

Killy-fish rippled the road ditch, a diminutive tempest, as the carriage and the hoof beats of the horses slightly shook the ground in passing.

Without further sign from the Doc, John turned to the left at Mooney's halfway house and continued up the road. Along this road, so I have been told—and the house is still there—lived a woman who kept a regular hangout for Rivers. It might have been a common joint, I don't know, but that isn't the way I heard it.

Certainly it was in an unusually isolated location, one of the old places, like the mansions on the hill only smaller, more suitable to farming. She was a descendant of the original builders.

Hello, Jimmie, how are you? Come in, bring your cigar with you.

That's the way it began. That's the way it always began. He would be just starting a stogie.

Hello, Doc, how's the boy? would say her brother. He ran the farm for her since her husband walked out.

I hope he's sunk in the mud, was all she'd say when that subject came up for comment.

By this time John would have turned the horses around and be on his way home.

The house is still there in much the same condition as formerly, quite close to the road with the farm buildings piled up in the rear, mostly given over to pigeons now. Rivers was known to about live there at one time.

Anyhow, you could see the chickens walking around in the yard all day. They had a colored man who had grown up on the place to take care of the few remnants of the garden that still remained; he went by the windows toward the middle of the afternoon and you could hear him call the chickens and see them run.

What could the attraction have been? Just one thing. Someone else, something else, to take him out of it. She was a good drinker. She gave him a rest.

But certainly she had, and I guess he knew it pretty well too, quite a bit put away. You know how these old farmers sometimes are. The increase in land valuations grow to be enormous; they have no need to move to become wealthy selling off sections of the original farm to the Polacks and promoters. She was one of those, hearing of cities and seeing trains crawling right before their eyes night and day, who remain isolated—peculiarly childish. Hot and eccentric.

Rivers would find an abandoned corner like that to wander into.

The drink alone would have been enough in itself to attract him. But she was a woman. The loafers around the bar at Donnelley's were all right. She was a woman. Maybe he never thought much of that but she *was* just the same.

Plenty of woman.

His sensitiveness, his refinement, his delicacy—found perhaps a release in this backhanded fashion. Can you believe it?

Jesus, she could put up a fight if she wanted to.

She didn't give a good God damn for the whole blankin' world—if you could believe her when she was drunk. And she said it—many times—to her brother and the Doc who put her to bed before he went home.

Then he'd have to come back next day and get her out of it—if they could find him. That's how they came to call him the first time.

Come on, Jimmie, let's get married, she would say.

Sure, where's the priest? and you could tell by his voice that you wouldn't ask him that many times before you wouldn't see him again ever.

Then he quit her. They'd drunk up all her booze, or her brother put a stop to the affair but, anyway, he quit.

I saw her just once many years later when she was completely abandoned.

It was the night we had her up at the Police Station for running through the gates at the railroad crossing. There were five in the car. It was a marvel the train didn't crash them. I was police physician at that time. They wanted me to pass on her, whether or not she was drunk.

She shoved her face close up against mine and yelled at me: Have you a sister, have you a brother? Then tell me I'm drunk. Her breath reeked half across the room. Look at me! Then she went off into an unrepeatable string of filth and profanity. And that's what I think of youse. I said it. You heard me.

It was the first and only time I saw her—if indeed she was the one of whom I had heard spoken. She must, at least, have been a good bit more attractive formerly.

As far as I know, he took all the ordinary hypnotics— morphine, heroin and cocaine also. What dose he ever got up to, it's hard to say. I've seen three grains of morphine do no more than make a woman—lying in a maternity ward—normally quiet.

Of course, it got him finally; he began to slip badly in the latter years, made pitiful blunders. But this final phase was marked by that curious idolatry that sometimes attracts people to a man by the very danger of his name. It lived again in the way many people, not all, still clung to Rivers the more he went down and down.

They seemed to recreate him in their minds, the beloved scapegoat of their own aberrant desires—and believed that he alone could cure them.

He became a legend and indulged himself the more.

But he did do awful things. It is said that he had made the remark that all a woman needed was half her organs— the others were just a surgeon's opportunity. Half the girls of Creston were without the half of theirs, through his offices, if you could believe his story.

It amused me to hear Jack Hardt describe how old Rivers would drop in at their tiny farm out in the reeds along the turnpike by the cedar swamp; a very small place, just a few feet of ground rescued from the bog with room only for a chicken coop, a doghouse, a barn and a hay rick. The old man used to make a fairly decent living off it, though, formerly, selling salt hay. I remember Jack's telling me how the hired men would sleep on the hay in winter with the snow seeping through on them between the boards and the one in the middle sweating from the body heat of his companions.

Rivers was a frequent caller at that place and always welcome there. The boy knew him well. The Doc would go out into the old privy they had at the back of the yard and stay there for an hour or more sometimes. The kids would go out and peep at him asleep on the seat.

He'd do the same anywhere. One woman up on the hill who did not know him well had him in to see her. He asked if she had a spare room with a bed in it. She said, Yes, not thinking what was in his mind. He went in and stayed. She was frightened to death. She frantically called up several friends but she could interest no one. Rivers had lain down on the bed and there he slept until nearly five in the afternoon, when his man called to fetch him.

The man knew to a dot when to come. In the morning after Rivers failed to show up, he had simply driven off. When the drug had worn itself out, he was there.

Rivers just got up, said nothing, and went home.

Sometimes, though, it was not so harmless.

How did he get away with it?

It is a little inherent in medicine itself—mystery, necromancy, cures—charms of all sorts, and he knew and practiced this black art. Toward the last of his life he had a crooked eye and was thought to be somewhat touched.

An impressionable lady once caused him an unpleasant half hour because of these things. It appears that he had for some reason taken a flier with her in hypnotism and unexpectedly succeeded in putting her under. But he could not rouse her to normal consciousness again when he was through with the experiment and finally becoming himself frightened, called frantically for his friend Willie to come down and help him get her out of the office. The two men, no doubt as mystified as the patient herself at the turn of

affairs, were thoroughly scared before—after great efforts
—they succeeded in bringing the lady to herself once more.

My wife remembers him staring in at our front door
through the screen. He had come to ask if I had any death
certificates. She couldn't tell which eye was looking at her.
But she noted the wistfulness of his stoop, his eager smile,
his voice, his gestures. She felt sorry for him.

But most feared him—in short, dared not attack him even
when they knew he had really killed someone.

A cure for disease? He knew what that amounted to. For
of what shall one be cured? Work, in this case, through
sheer intuitive ability flooded him under. Drugs righted him.

Frightened, under stress, the heart beats faster, the blood
is driven to the extremities of the nerves, floods the centers
of action and a man feels in a flame. That's what Rivers
wanted, must have wanted. The reaction from such a state
required its tonics also.

That awful fever of overwork which we feel especially in
the United States—he had it. A trembling in the arms and
thighs, a tightness of the neck and in the head above the
eyes—fast breath, vague pains in the muscles and in the feet.
Followed by an orgasm, crashing the job through, putting
it over in a fever heat. Then the feeling of looseness afterward. Not pleasant. But there it is. Then cigarettes, a shot
of gin. And that's all there is to it. Women the same, more
and more.

He had no time, had to be fast, he had to improvise and
did—to a marvel.

When a street laborer was clipped once by a trolley car,
his arm almost severed near the shoulder, Rivers was the
first to get there. Such cases were always his particular
delight. With one look he took in the situation as usual,
made up his mind, and remarking that the arm could be of
no possible further use to the man, amputated it there and
then—with a pair of bandage scissors.

Such deeds took the popular fancy and the rumor of them spread like magic.

It's funny too, the answer of the Sisters in the hospital when some of the doctors wanted to prevent him from operating there—principally because he would pass out, finally, in the middle of a case and someone else would have to go in and clean it up for him. The Sisters would say in reply to such complainers: What do you wish us to do? So long as people go to the man, we will keep a bed free for them here. Do you want us to go back on them?

It was an unanswerable argument.

He was one of the few that ever in these parts knew the meaning of all, to give himself completely. He never asked why, never gave a damn, never thought there was anything else. He was like that, things had an absolute value for him.

But one of the younger doctors, a first-rate physician who began practicing in the town a month or two prior to my own arrival, had it in for Rivers. My wife would sometimes say to me, If you know he is killing people, why do you doctors not get together and have his license taken away from him?

I would answer that I didn't know. I doubted that we could prove anything. No one wanted to try.

Dr. Grimley, though, did want to do something that day.

He had had a Hungarian girl, who was scared as hell of the knife, under his care with a strangulated hernia. Grimley tried his best to reduce it but without success. He knew the danger and urged her by every means at his command to go to the hospital and have the operation. She refused.

He very properly told her that, unless she did as he told her, he would no longer handle the case and that she would die.

The next day she called him again. As soon as he entered the room, he could see that it was all over. She had called in Rivers. He had told her that he could cure her. God knows what condition he was in at the time. He pressed upon the sac until it burst. The next day she died.

Grimley was wild. I met him at the corner by the drug store. Though a very quiet man he was fairly foaming at the mouth. He wanted to have Rivers arrested, he wanted to have him prosecuted for malpractice and to put him out of the way once and for all—said he'd do it.

He never did.

In reality, it was a population in despair, out of hand, out of discipline, driven about by each other blindly, believing in the miraculous, the drunken, as it may be. Here was, to many, though they are diminishing fast, something before which they could worship, a local shrine, all there was left, a measure of the poverty which surrounded them. They believed in him: Rivers, drunk or sober. It is a plaintive, failing story.

Typical of their behavior is the tale of a very sober and canny butcher whom I know well who had a small daughter that had what seemed to me to be typical epileptic fits. They called me in and I told the parents there was little I could do for them.

Later I saw them again and they confessed to me frankly that they had taken the child to Dr. Rivers. I wished them luck.

A year later, I had occasion to talk to them again of the child. She had not had a convulsion for several months. Rivers had cured her. How, I do not know.

Yes, the father said, it took us quite a while to get him working but once he really got his mind down on the case, it didn't take him long till he had her where he wanted her. They believed it and it was so.

People sought him out, they'd wait months for him finally —though he did, of his own volition, give up maternity cases toward the end. When everyone else failed, they believed he'd see them through: a powerful fetish. He would save them.

The end was recounted to me by a young patient of mine, a teller in the bank. His father had always had Rivers. So when the old man fell and broke his arm, they called up the Doc who came and deliberately hopped himself up right before the patient—undisguisedly, so indifferent had he become.

That finished it. It was the look in his eyes. He's crazy, said the patient. Take him away. I don't want him fooling around me. I'll get another doctor.

But it would not be just to say that this was really the end, for that gives a wrong impression. Rivers was through, yes, in some ways, but he did not quit by any means. The truth is that during his last years he bought a good-sized lot on the square before the Municipal Building in the center of town. Here he built a fine house, had a large garden, lawns and a double garage, where he kept two cars always ready for service.

Here he continued to practice for several years while his wife bred small dogs—Blue Poms, I think, for her amusement and for sale, one or more of which Rivers would often take out in the car with him on his calls, holding them on his lap, for in those days he himself never sat at the wheel.

The Girl with a Pimply Face

ONE OF THE LOCAL DRUGGISTS sent in the call: 50 Summer St.,
second floor, the door to the left. It's a baby they've just
brought from the hospital. Pretty bad condition I should
imagine. Do you want to make it? I think they've had somebody else but don't like him, he added as an afterthought.

It was half past twelve. I was just sitting down to lunch.
Can't they wait till after office hours?

Oh I guess so. But they're foreigners and you know how
they are. Make it as soon as you can. I guess the baby's
pretty bad.

It was two-thirty when I got to the place, over a shop in
the business part of town. One of those street doors between
plate glass show windows. A narrow entry with smashed
mail boxes on one side and a dark stair leading straight up.
I'd been to the address a number of times during the past
years to see various people who had lived there.

Going up I found no bell so I rapped vigorously on the
wavy-glass door-panel to the left. I knew it to be the door
to the kitchen, which occupied the rear of that apartment.

Come in, said a loud childish voice.

I opened the door and saw a lank haired girl of about fifteen standing chewing gum and eyeing me curiously from
beside the kitchen table. The hair was coal black and one
of her eyelids drooped a little as she spoke. Well, what do
you want? she said. Boy, she was tough and no kidding but
I fell for her immediately. There was that hard, straight
thing about her that in itself gives an impression of ex-
cellence.

42

I'm the doctor, I said.

Oh, you're the doctor. The baby's inside. She looked at me. Want to see her?

Sure, that's what I came for. Where's your mother?

She's out. I don't know when she's coming back. But you can take a look at the baby if you want to.

All right. Let's see her.

She led the way into the bedroom, toward the front of the flat, one of the unlit rooms, the only windows being those in the kitchen and along the facade of the building.

There she is.

I looked on the bed and saw a small face, emaciated but quiet, unnaturally quiet, sticking out of the upper end of a tightly rolled bundle made by the rest of the baby encircled in a blue cotton blanket. The whole wasn't much larger than a good sized loaf of rye bread. Hands and everything were rolled up. Just the yellowish face showed, tightly hatted and framed around by a corner of the blanket.

What's the matter with her, I asked.

I dunno, said the girl as fresh as paint and seeming about as indifferent as though it had been no relative of hers instead of her sister. I looked at my informer very much amused and she looked back at me, chewing her gum vigorously, standing there her feet well apart. She cocked her head to one side and gave it to me straight in the eye, as much as to say, Well? I looked back at her. She had one of those small, squeezed up faces, snub nose, overhanging eyebrows, low brow and a terrible complexion, pimply and coarse.

When's your mother coming back do you *think*, I asked again.

Maybe in an hour. But maybe you'd better come some time when my father's here. He talks English. He ought to come in around five I guess.

But can't you tell me something about the baby? I hear it's been sick. Does it have a fever?

I dunno.

But has it diarrhoea, are its movements green?

Sure, she said, I guess so. It's been in the hospital but it got worse so my father brought it home today.

What are they feeding it?

A bottle. You can see that yourself. There it is.

There was a cold bottle of half finished milk lying on the coverlet the nipple end of it fallen behind the baby's head.

How old is she? It's a girl, did you say?

Yeah, it's a girl.

Your sister?

Sure. Want to examine it?

No thanks, I said. For the moment at least I had lost all interest in the baby. This young kid in charge of the house did something to me that I liked. She was just a child but nobody was putting anything over on her if she knew it, yet the real thing about her was the complete lack of the rotten smell of a liar. She wasn't in the least presumptive. Just straight.

But after all she wasn't such a child. She had breasts you knew would be like small stones to the hand, good muscular arms and fine hard legs. Her bare feet were stuck into broken down leather sandals such as you see worn by children at the beach in summer. She was heavily tanned too, wherever her skin showed. Just one of the kids you'll find loafing around the pools they have outside towns and cities everywhere these days. A tough little nut finding her own way in the world.

What's the matter with your legs? I asked. They were bare and covered with scabby sores.

Poison ivy, she answered, pulling up her skirts to show me.

Gee, but you ought to seen it two days ago. This ain't nothing. You're a doctor. What can I do for it?

Let's see, I said.

She put her leg up on a chair. It had been badly bitten by mosquitoes, as I saw the thing, but she insisted on poison ivy. She had torn at the affected places with her finger nails and that's what made it look worse.

Oh that's not so bad, I said, if you'll only leave it alone and stop scratching it.

Yeah, I know that but I can't. Scratching's the only thing makes it feel better.

What's that on your foot.

Where? looking.

That big brown spot there on the back of your foot.

Dirt I guess. Her gum chewing never stopped and her fixed defensive non-expression never changed.

Why don't you wash it?

I do. Say, what could I do for my face?

I looked at it closely. You have what they call acne, I told her. All those blackheads and pimples you see there, well, let's see, the first thing you ought to do, I suppose is to get some good soap.

What kind of soap? Lifebuoy?

No. I'd suggest one of those cakes of Lux. Not the flakes but the cake.

Yeah, I know, she said. Three for seventeen.

Use it. Use it every morning. Bathe your face in very hot water. You know, until the skin is red from it. That's to bring the blood up to the skin. Then take a piece of ice. You have ice, haven't you?

Sure, we have ice.

Hold it in a face cloth—or whatever you have—and rub that all over your face. Do that right after you've washed it in the very hot water—before it has cooled. Rub the ice all over. And do it every day—for a month. Your skin will improve. If you like, you can take some cold cream once in a while, not much, just a little and rub that in last of all, if your face feels too dry.

Will that help me?

If you stick to it, it'll help you.

All right.

There's a lotion I could give you to use along with that. Remind me of it when I come back later. Why aren't you in school?

Agh, I'm not going any more. They can't make me. Can they?

They can try.

How can they? I know a girl thirteen that don't go and they can't make her either.

Don't you want to learn things?

I know enough already.

Going to get a job?

I got a job. Here. I been helping the Jews across the hall. They give me three fifty a week—all summer.

Good for you, I said. Think your father'll be here around five?

Guess so. He ought to be.

I'll come back then. Make it all the same call.

All right, she said, looking straight at me and chewing her gum as vigorously as ever.

Just then a little blond haired thing of about seven came in through the kitchen and walked to me looking curiously at my satchel and then at the baby.

What are you, a doctor?

See you later, I said to the older girl and went out.

At five-thirty I once more climbed the wooden stairs after passing two women at the street entrance who looked me up and down from where they were leaning on the brick wall of the building talking.

This time a woman's voice said, Come in, when I knocked on the kitchen door.

It was the mother. She was impressive, a bulky woman, growing toward fifty, in a black dress, with lank graying hair and a long seamed face. She stood by the enameled kitchen table. A younger, plumpish woman with blond hair, well cared for and in a neat house dress—as if she had dolled herself up for the occasion—was standing beside her.

The small blank child was there too and the older girl, behind the others, overshadowed by her mother, the two older women at least a head taller than she. No one spoke.

Hello, I said to the girl I had been talking to earlier. She didn't answer me.

Doctor, began the mother, save my baby. She very sick. The woman spoke with a thick, heavy voice and seemed overcome with grief and apprehension. Doctor! Doctor! she all but wept.

All right, I said to cut the woman short, let's take a look at her first.

So everybody headed toward the front of the house, the mother in the lead. As they went I lagged behind to speak to the second woman, the interpreter. What happened?

The baby was not doing so well. So they took it to the hospital to see if the doctors there could help it. But it got worse. So her husband took it out this morning. It looks bad to me.

Yes, said the mother who had overheard us. Me got seven children. One daughter married. This my baby, pointing to the child on the bed. And she wiped her face with the back of her hand. This baby no do good. Me almost crazy. Don't know who can help. What doctor, I don't know. Somebody tell me take to hospital. I think maybe do some good. Five days she there. Cost me two dollar every day. Ten dollar. I no got money. And when I see my baby, she worse. She look dead. I can't leave she there. No. No. I say to everybody, no. I take she home. Doctor, you save my baby. I pay you. I pay you everything—

Wait a minute, wait a minute, I said. Then I turned to the other woman. What happened?

The baby got like a diarrhoea in the hospital. And she was all dirty when they went to see her. They got all excited—

All sore behind, broke in the mother—

The younger woman said a few words to her in some language that sounded like Russian but it didn't stop her—

No. No. I send she to hospital. And when I see my baby like that I can't leave she there. My babies no that way. Never, she emphasized. Never! I take she home.

Take your time, I said. Take off her clothes. Everything off. This is a regular party. It's warm enough in here. Does she vomit?

She no eat. How she can vomit? said the mother.

But the other woman contradicted her. Yes, she was vomiting in the hospital, the nurse said.

It happens that this September we had been having a lot of such cases in my hospital also, an infectious diarrhoea which practically all the children got when they came in from any cause. I supposed that this was what happened to this child. No doubt it had been in a bad way before that, improper feeding, etc., etc. And then when they took it in there, for whatever had been the matter with it, the diarrhoea had developed. These things sometimes don't turn out so well. Lucky, no doubt, that they had brought it home when they did. I told them so, explaining at the same time: One nurse for ten or twenty babies, they do all they can but you can't run and change the whole ward every five minutes. But the infant looked too lifeless for that only to be the matter with it.

You want all clothes off, asked the mother again, hesitating and trying to keep the baby covered with the cotton blanket while undressing it.

Everything off, I said.

There it lay, just skin and bones with a round fleshless head at the top and the usual pot belly you find in such cases.

Look, said the mother, tilting the infant over on its right side with her big hands so that I might see the reddened buttocks. What kind of nurse that. My babies never that way.

Take your time, take your time, I told her. That's not bad. And it wasn't either. Any child with loose movements might have had the same half an hour after being cared for. Come on. Move away, I said and give me a chance. She kept hovering over the baby as if afraid I might expose it.

It had no temperature. There was no rash. The mouth was in reasonably good shape. Eyes, ears negative. The moment I put my stethescope to the little boney chest, however, the whole thing became clear. The infant had a severe congenital heart defect, a roar when you listened over the heart that meant, to put it crudely, that she was no good, never would be.

The mother was watching me. I straightened up and looking at her told her plainly: She's got a bad heart.

That was the sign for tears. The big woman cried while she spoke. Doctor, she pleaded in blubbering anguish, save my baby.

I'll help her, I said, but she's got a bad heart. That will never be any better. But I knew perfectly well she wouldn't pay the least attention to what I was saying.

I give you anything, she went on. I pay you. I pay you twenty dollar. Doctor, you fix my baby. You good doctor. You fix.

All right, all right, I said. What are you feeding it?

They told me and it was a ridiculous formula, unboiled besides. I regulated it properly for them and told them how to proceed to make it up. Have you got enough bottles, I asked the young girl.

Sure, we got bottles, she told me.

O.K., then go ahead.

You think you cure she? The mother with her long, tearful face was at me again, so different from her tough female fifteen-year-old.

You do what I tell you for three days, I said, and I'll come back and see how you're getting on.

Tank you, doctor, so much. I pay you. I got today no

money. I pay ten dollar to hospital. They cheat me. I got no more money. I pay you Friday when my husband get pay. You save my baby.

Boy! what a woman. I couldn't get away.

She my baby, doctor. I no want to lose. Me got seven children—

Yes, you told me.

But this my baby. You understand. She very sick. You good doctor—

Oh my God! To get away from her I turned again to the kid. You better get going after more bottles before the stores close. I'll come back Friday morning.

How about that stuff for my face you were gonna give me.

That's right. Wait a minute. And I sat down on the edge of the bed to write out a prescription for some lotio alba comp. such as we use in acne. The two older women looked at me in astonishment—wondering, I suppose, how I knew the girl. I finished writing the thing and handed it to her. Sop it on your face at bedtime, I said, and let it dry on. Don't get it into your eyes.

No, I won't.

I'll see you in a couple of days, I said to them all.

Doctor! the old woman was still after me. You come back. I pay you. But all a time short. Always tomorrow come milk man. Must pay rent, must pay coal. And no got money. Too much work. Too much wash. Too much cook. Nobody help. I don't know what's a matter. This door, doctor, this door. This house make sick. Make sick.

Do the best I can, I said as I was leaving.

The girl followed on the stairs. How much is this going to cost, she asked shrewdly holding the prescription.

Not much, I said, and then started to think. Tell them you only got half a dollar. Tell them I said that's all it's worth.

Is that right, she said.

Absolutely. Don't pay a cent more for it.

Say, you're all right, she looked at me appreciatively.

Have you got half a dollar.

Sure. Why not.

What's it all about, my wife asked me in the evening. She had heard about the case. Gee! I sure met a wonderful girl, I told her.

What! another?

Some tough baby. I'm crazy about her. Talk about straight stuff . . . And I recounted to her the sort of case it was and what I had done. The mother's an odd one too. I don't quite make her out.

Did they pay you?

No. I don't suppose they have any cash.

Going back?

Sure. Have to.

Well, I don't see why you have to do all this charity work. Now that's a case you should report to the Emergency Relief. You'll get at least two dollars a call from them.

But the father has a job, I understand. That counts me out.

What sort of a job?

I dunno. Forgot to ask.

What's the baby's name so I can put it in the book?

Damn it. I never thought to ask them that either. I think they must have told me but I can't remember it. Some kind of a Russian name—

You're the limit. Dumbbell, she laughed. Honestly—Who are they anyhow.

You know, I think it must be that family Kate was telling us about. Don't you remember. The time the little kid was playing there one afternoon after school, fell down the front steps and knocked herself senseless.

I don't recall.

Sure you do. That's the family. I get it now. Kate took the brat down there in a taxi and went up with her to see that everything was all right. Yop, that's it. The old woman took the older kid by the hair, because she hadn't watched her sister. And what a beating she gave her. Don't you remember Kate telling us afterward. She thought the old woman was going to murder the child she screamed and threw her around so. Some old gal. You can see they're all afraid of her. What a world. I suppose the damned brat drives her cuckoo. But boy, how she clings to that baby.

The last hope, I suppose, said my wife.

Yeah, and the worst bet in the lot. There's a break for you.

She'll love it just the same.

More, usually.

Three days later I called at the flat again. Come in. This time a resonant male voice. I entered, keenly interested.

By the same kitchen table stood a short, thickset man in baggy working pants and a heavy cotton undershirt. He seemed to have the stability of a cube placed on one of its facets, a smooth, highly colored Slavic face, long black moustaches and widely separated, perfectly candid blue eyes. His black hair, glossy and profuse stood out carelessly all over his large round head. By his look he reminded me at once of his blond haired daughter, absolutely unruffled. The shoulders of an ox. You the doctor, he said. Come in.

The girl and the small child were beside him, the mother was in the bedroom.

The baby no better. Won't eat, said the man in answer to my first question.

How are its bowels?

Not so bad.

Does it vomit?

No.

Then it is better, I objected. But by this time the mother had heard us talking and came in. She seemed worse than the last time. Absolutely inconsolable. Doctor! Doctor! she came up to me.

Somewhat irritated I put her aside and went in to the
baby. Of course it was better, much better. So I told them.
But the heart, naturally was the same.

How she heart? the mother pressed me eagerly. Today
little better?

I started to explain things to the man who was standing
back giving his wife precedence but as soon as she got the
drift of what I was saying she was all over me again and the
tears began to pour. There was no use my talking. Doctor,
you good doctor. You do something fix my baby. And
before I could move she took my left hand in both hers and
kissed it through her tears. As she did so I realized finally
that she had been drinking.

I turned toward the man, looking a good bit like the sun
at noonday and as indifferent, then back to the woman and
I felt deeply sorry for her.

Then, not knowing why I said it nor of whom, precisely
I was speaking, I felt myself choking inwardly with the
words: Hell! God damn it. The sons of bitches. Why do
these things have to be?

The next morning as I came into the coat room at the
hospital there were several of the visiting staff standing
there with their cigarettes, talking. It was about a hunting
dog belonging to one of the doctors. It had come down with
distemper and seemed likely to die.

I called up half a dozen vets around here, one of them was
saying. I even called up the one in your town, he added
turning to me as I came in. And do you know how much
they wanted to charge me for giving the serum to that
animal?

Nobody answered.

They had the nerve to want to charge me five dollars a
shot for it. Can you beat that? Five dollars a shot.

Did you give them the job, someone spoke up facetiously.

Did I? I should say I did not, the first answered. But can

you beat that. Why we're nothing but a lot of slop-heels compared to those guys. We deserve to starve.

Get it out of them, someone rasped, kidding. That's the stuff.

Then the original speaker went on, buttonholing me as some of the others faded from the room. Did you ever see practice so rotten. By the way, I was called over to your town about a week ago to see a kid I delivered up here during the summer. Do you know anything about the case?

I probably got them on my list, I said. Russians?

Yeah, I thought as much. Has a job as a road worker or something. Said they couldn't pay me. Well, I took the trouble of going up to your court house and finding out what he was getting. Eighteen dollars a week. Just the type. And they had the nerve to tell me they couldn't pay me.

She told me ten.

She's a liar.

Natural maternal instinct, I guess.

Whisky appetite, if you should ask me.

Same thing.

O.K. buddy. Only I'm telling you. And did I tell *them*. They'll never call me down there again, believe me. I had that much satisfaction out of them anyway. You make 'em pay you. Don't you do anything for them unless they do. He's paid by the county. I tell you if I had taxes to pay down there I'd go and take it out of his salary.

You and how many others?

Say, they're bad actors, that crew. Do you know what they really do with their money? Whisky. Now I'm telling you. That old woman is the slickest customer you ever saw. She's drunk all the time. Didn't you notice it?

Not while I was there.

Don't you let them put any of that sympathy game over on you. Why they tell me she leaves that baby lying on the bed all day long screaming its lungs out until the neighbors complain to the police about it. I'm not lying to you.

Yeah, the old skate's got nerves, you can see that. I can imagine she's a bugger when she gets going.

But what about the young girl, I asked weakly. She seems like a pretty straight kid.

My confrere let out a wild howl. That thing! You mean that pimply faced little bitch. Say, if I had my way I'd run her out of the town tomorrow morning. There's about a dozen wise guys on her trail every night in the week. Ask the cops. Just ask them. They know. Only nobody wants to bring in a complaint. They say you'll stumble over her on the roof, behind the stairs anytime at all. Boy, they sure took you in.

Yes, I suppose they did, I said.

But the old woman's the ringleader. She's got the brains. Take my advice and make them pay.

The last time I went I heard the, Come in! from the front of the house. The fifteen-year-old was in there at the window in a rocking chair with the tightly wrapped baby in her arms. She got up. Her legs were bare to the hips. A powerful little animal.

What are you doing? Going swimming? I asked.

Naw, that's my gym suit. What the kids wear for Physical Training in school.

How's the baby?

She's all right.

Do you mean it?

Sure, she eats fine now.

Tell your mother to bring it to the office some day so I can weigh it. The food'll need increasing in another week or two anyway.

I'll tell her.

How's your face?

Gettin' better.

My God, it *is*, I said. And it was much better. Going back to school now?

Yeah, I had tuh.

The Use of Force

THEY WERE new patients to me, all I had was the name, Olson. Please come down as soon as you can, my daughter is very sick.

When I arrived I was met by the mother, a big startled looking woman, very clean and apologetic who merely said, Is this the doctor? and let me in. In the back, she added. You must excuse us, doctor, we have her in the kitchen where it is warm. It is very damp here sometimes.

The child was fully dressed and sitting on her father's lap near the kitchen table. He tried to get up, but I motioned for him not to bother, took off my overcoat and started to look things over. I could see that they were all very nervous, eyeing me up and down distrustfully. As often, in such cases, they weren't telling me more than they had to, it was up to me to tell them; that's why they were spending three dollars on me.

The child was fairly eating me up with her cold, steady eyes, and no expression to her face whatever. She did not move and seemed, inwardly, quiet; an unusually attractive little thing, and as strong as a heifer in appearance. But her face was flushed, she was breathing rapidly, and I realized that she had a high fever. She had magnificent blonde hair, in profusion. One of those picture children often reproduced in advertising leaflets and the photogravure sections of the Sunday papers.

She's had a fever for three days, began the father and we don't know what it comes from. My wife has given her things, you know, like people do, but it don't do no good.

And there's been a lot of sickness around. So we tho't you'd better look her over and tell us what is the matter.

As doctors often do I took a trial shot at it as a point of departure. Has she had a sore throat?

Both parents answered me together, No . . . No, she says her throat don't hurt her.

Does your throat hurt you? added the mother to the child. But the little girl's expression didn't change nor did she move her eyes from my face.

Have you looked?

I tried to, said the mother, but I couldn't see.

As it happens we had been having a number of cases of diphtheria in the school to which this child went during that month and we were all, quite apparently, thinking of that, though no one had as yet spoken of the thing.

Well, I said, suppose we take a look at the throat first. I smiled in my best professional manner and asking for the child's first name I said, come on, Mathilda, open your mouth and let's take a look at your throat.

Nothing doing.

Aw, come on, I coaxed, just open your mouth wide and let me take a look. Look, I said opening both hands wide, I haven't anything in my hands. Just open up and let me see.

Such a nice man, put in the mother. Look how kind he is to you. Come on, do what he tells you to. He won't hurt you.

At that I ground my teeth in disgust. If only they wouldn't use the word "hurt" I might be able to get somewhere. But I did not allow myself to be hurried or disturbed but speaking quietly and slowly I approached the child again.

As I moved my chair a little nearer suddenly with one cat-like movement both her hands clawed instinctively for my eyes and she almost reached them too. In fact she knocked my glasses flying and they fell, though unbroken, several feet away from me on the kitchen floor.

Both the mother and father almost turned themselves

inside out in embarrassment and apology. You bad girl, said
the mother, taking her and shaking her by one arm. Look
what you've done. The nice man . . .

For heaven's sake, I broke in. Don't call me a nice man
to her. I'm here to look at her throat on the chance that
she might have diphtheria and possibly die of it. But that's
nothing to her. Look here, I said to the child, we're going
to look at your throat. You're old enough to understand
what I'm saying. Will you open it now by yourself or shall
we have to open it for you?

Not a move. Even her expression hadn't changed. Her
breaths however were coming faster and faster. Then the
battle began. I had to do it. I had to have a throat culture
for her own protection. But first I told the parents that it
was entirely up to them. I explained the danger but said
that I would not insist on a throat examination so long as
they would take the responsibility.

If you don't do what the doctor says you'll have to go to
the hospital, the mother admonished her severely.

Oh yeah? I had to smile to myself. After all, I had already
fallen in love with the savage brat, the parents were con-
temptible to me. In the ensuing struggle they grew more and
more abject, crushed, exhausted while she surely rose to
magnificent heights of insane fury of effort bred of her
terror of me.

The father tried his best, and he was a big man but the
fact that she was his daughter, his shame at her behavior and
his dread of hurting her made him release her just at the
critical moment several times when I had almost achieved
success, till I wanted to kill him. But his dread also that
she might have diphtheria made him tell me to go on, go
on though he himself was almost fainting, while the mother
moved back and forth behind us raising and lowering her
hands in an agony of apprehension.

Put her in front of you on your lap, I ordered, and hold
both her wrists.

But as soon as he did the child let out a scream. Don't, you're hurting me. Let go of my hands. Let them go I tell you. Then she shrieked terrifyingly, hysterically. Stop it! Stop it! You're killing me!

Do you think she can stand it, doctor! said the mother.

You get out, said the husband to his wife. Do you want her to die of diphtheria?

Come on now, hold her, I said.

Then I grasped the child's head with my left hand and tried to get the wooden tongue depressor between her teeth. She fought, with clenched teeth, desperately! But now I also had grown furious—at a child. I tried to hold myself down but I couldn't. I know how to expose a throat for inspection. And I did my best. When finally I got the wooden spatula behind the last teeth and just the point of it into the mouth cavity, she opened up for an instant but before I could see anything she came down again and gripping the wooden blade between her molars she reduced it to splinters before I could get it out again.

Aren't you ashamed, the mother yelled at her. Aren't you ashamed to act like that in front of the doctor?

Get me a smooth-handled spoon of some sort, I told the mother. We're going through with this. The child's mouth was already bleeding. Her tongue was cut and she was screaming in wild hysterical shrieks. Perhaps I should have desisted and come back in an hour or more. No doubt it would have been better. But I have seen at least two children lying dead in bed of neglect in such cases, and feeling that I must get a diagnosis now or never I went at it again. But the worst of it was that I too had got beyond reason. I could have torn the child apart in my own fury and enjoyed it. It was a pleasure to attack her. My face was burning with it.

The damned little brat must be protected against her own idiocy, one says to one's self at such times. Others must be protected against her. It is social necessity. And all these things are true. But a blind fury, a feeling of adult shame, bred of a longing for muscular release are the operatives. One goes on to the end.

In a final unreasoning assault I overpowered the child's neck and jaws. I forced the heavy silver spoon back of her teeth and down her throat till she gagged. And there it was —both tonsils covered with membrane. She had fought valiantly to keep me from knowing her secret. She had been hiding that sore throat for three days at least and lying to her parents in order to escape just such an outcome as this.

Now truly she *was* furious. She had been on the defensive before but now she attacked. Tried to get off her father's lap and fly at me while tears of defeat blinded her eyes.

A Night in June

I WAS a young man then—full of information and tenderness. It was her first baby. She lived just around the corner from her present abode, one room over a small general store kept by an old man.

It was a difficult forceps delivery and I lost the child, to my disgust; though without nurse, anesthetist, or even enough hot water in the place, I shouldn't have been overmuch blamed. I must have been fairly able not to have done worse. But I won a friend and I found another—to admire, a sort of love for the woman.

She was slightly older than her husband, a heavy-looking Italian boy. Both were short. A peasant woman who could scarcely talk a word of English, being recently come from the other side, a woman of great simplicity of character—docility, patience, with a fine direct look in her grey eyes. And courageous. Devoted to her instincts and convictions and to me.

Sometimes she'd cry out at her husband, as I got to know her later, with some high pitched animalistic sound when he would say something her in Italian that I couldn't understand and I knew that she was holding out for me.

Usually though, she said very little, looking me straight in the eye with a smile, her voice pleasant and candid though I could scarcely understand her few broken words. Her sentences were seldom more than three or four words long. She always acted as though I must naturally know what was in her mind and her smile with a shrug always won me.

Apart from the second child, born a year after the first,

during the absence of the family from town for a short time, I had delivered Angelina of all her children. This one would make my eighth attendance on her, her ninth labor.

Three A.M., June the 10th, I noticed the calendar as I flashed on the light in my office to pick up my satchel, the same, by the way, my uncle had given me when I graduated from Medical School. One gets not to deliver women at home nowadays. The hospital is the place for it. The equipment is far better.

Smiling, I picked up the relic from where I had tossed it two or three years before under a table in my small laboratory hoping never to have to use it again. In it I found a brand new hypodermic syringe with the manufacturer's name still shiny with black enamel on the barrel. Also a pair of curved scissors I had been looking for for the last three years, thinking someone had stolen them.

I dusted off the top of the Lysol bottle when I took it from the shelf and quickly checking on the rest of my necessities, I went off, without a coat or necktie, wearing the same shirt I had had on during the day preceding, soiled but—better so.

It was a beautiful June night. The lighted clock in the tower over the factory said 3:20. The clock in the facade of the Trust Company across the track said it also. Paralleling the railroad I recognized the squat figure of the husband returning home ahead of me—whistling as he walked. I put my hand out of the car in sign of recognition and kept on, rounding the final triangular block a little way ahead to bring my car in to the right in front of the woman's house for parking.

The husband came up as I was trying to decide which of the two steep cobbled entry-ways to take. Got you up early, he said.

Where ya been? his sister said to him when we had got into the house from the rear.

I went down to the police to telephone, he said, that's the surest way.

I told you to go next door, you dope. What did you go away down there for? Leaving me here alone.

Aw, I didn't want to wake nobody up.

I got two calls, I broke in.

Yes, he went away and left me alone. I got scared so I waked him up anyway to call you.

The kitchen where we stood was lighted by a somewhat damaged Welsbach mantel gaslight. Everything was quiet. The husband took off his cap and sat along the wall. I put my satchel on the tubs and began to take things out.

There was just one sterile umbilical tie left, two, really, in the same envelope, as always, for possible twins, but that detail aside, everything was ample and in order. I complimented myself. Even the Argyrol was there, in tablet form, insuring the full potency of a fresh solution. Nothing so satisfying as a kit of any sort prepared and in order even when picked up in an emergency after an interval of years.

I selected out two artery clamps and two scissors. One thing, there'd be no need of sutures afterward in this case.

You want hot water?

Not yet, I said. Might as well take my shirt off, though. Which I did, throwing it on a kitchen chair and donning the usual light rubber apron.

I'm sorry we ain't got no light in there. The electricity is turned off. Do you think you can see with a candle?

Sure. Why not? But it was very dark in the room where the woman lay on a low double bed. A three-year-old boy was asleep on the sheet beside her. She wore an abbreviated nightgown, to her hips. Her short thick legs had, as I knew, bunches of large varicose veins about them like vines. Everything was clean and in order. The sister-in-law held the candle. Few words were spoken.

I made the examination and found the head high but the cervix fully dilated. Oh yeah. It often happens in women who have had many children; pendulous abdomen, lack of muscular power resulting in a slight misdirection of the forces of labor and the thing may go on for days.

When I finished, Angelina got up and sat on the edge of the bed. I went back to the kitchen, the candle following me, leaving the room dark again.

Do you need it any more? the sister-in-law said, I'll put it out.

Then the husband spoke up, Ain't you got but that one candle?

No, said the sister.

Why didn't you get some at the store when you woke him up; use your head.

The woman had the candle in a holder on the cold coal range. She leaned over to blow it out but misdirecting her aim, she had to blow three times to do it. Three or four times.

What's the matter? said her brother, getting weak? Old age counts, eh Doc? he said and got up finally to go out.

We could hear an engineer signaling outside in the still night—with short quick blasts of his whistle—very staccato —not, I suppose, to make any greater disturbance than necessary with people sleeping all about.

Later on the freights began to roar past shaking the whole house.

She doesn't seem to be having many strong pains, I said to my companion in the kitchen, for there wasn't a sound from the labor room and hadn't been for the past half hour.

She don't want to make no noise and wake the kids.

How old is the oldest now? I asked.

He's sixteen. The girl would have been eighteen this year. You know the first one you took from her.

Where are they all?

In there, with a nod of the head toward the other room of the apartment, such as it was, the first floor of an old two-story house, the whole thing perhaps twenty-five feet each way.

I sat in a straight chair by the kitchen table, my right arm, bare to the shoulder, resting on the worn oil cloth.

She says she wants an enema, said the woman. O.K. But I don't know how to give it to her. She ain't got a bed-pan or nothing. I don't want to get the bed all wet.

Has she had a movement today?

Yeah, but she thinks an enema will help her.

Well, have you got a bag?

Yeah, she says there's one here somewhere.

Get it. She's got a chamber pot here, hasn't she?

Sure.

So the woman got the equipment, a blue rubber douche bag, the rubber of it feeling rather stiff to the touch. She laid it on the stove in its open box and looked at it holding her hands out helplessly. I'm afraid, she said.

All right, you hold the candle. Mix up a little warm soapy water. We'll need some vaseline.

The woman called out to us where to find it, having overheard our conversation.

Lift up, till I put these newspapers under you, said my assistant. I don't want to wet the bed.

That's nothing, Angelina answered smiling. But she raised her buttocks high so we could fix her.

Returning ten minutes later to my chair, I saw the woman taking the pot out through the kitchen and upstairs to empty it. I crossed my legs, crossed my bare arms in my lap also and let my head fall forward. I must have slept, for when I opened my eyes again, both my legs and my arms were somewhat numb. I felt deliciously relaxed though somewhat bewildered. I must have snored, waking myself with a start. Everything was quiet as before. The peace of the room was unchanged. Delicious.

I heard the woman and her attendant making some slight sounds in the next room and went in to her.

Examining her, I found things unchanged. It was about half past four. What to do? Do you mind if I give you the needle? I asked her gently. We'd been through this many times before. She shrugged her shoulders as much as to say, It's up to you. So I gave her a few minims of pituitrin to intensify the strength of the pains. I was cautious since the practice is not without danger. It is possible to get a ruptured uterus where the muscle has been stretched by many pregnancies if one does not know what one is doing. Then I returned to the kitchen to wait once more.

This time I took out the obstetric gown I had brought with me, it was in a roll as it had come from the satchel, and covering it with my shirt to make a better surface and a little more bulk, I placed it at the edge of the table and leaning forward, laid my face sidewise upon it, my arms resting on the table before me, my nose and mouth at the table edge between my arms. I could breathe freely. It was a pleasant position and as I lay there content, I thought as I often do of what painting it was in which I had seen men sleeping that way.

Then I fell asleep and, in my half sleep began to argue with myself—or some imaginary power—of science and humanity. Our exaggerated ways will have to pull in their horns, I said. We've learned from one teacher and neglected another. Now that I'm older, I'm finding the older school.

The pituitary extract and other simple devices represent science. Science, I dreamed, has crowded the stage more than is necessary. The process of selection will simplify the application. It touches us too crudely now, all newness is over-complex. I couldn't tell whether I was asleep or awake.

But without science, without pituitrin, I'd be here till noon or maybe—what? Some others wouldn't wait so long but rush her now. A carefully guarded shot of pituitrin— ought to save her at least much exhaustion—if not more. But I don't want to have anything happen to her.

Now when I lifted my head, there was beginning to be a

little light outside. The woman was quiet. No progress. This time I increased the dose of pituitrin. She had stronger pains but without effect.

Maybe I'd better give you a still larger dose, I said. She made no demur. Well, let me see if I can help you first. I sat on the edge of the bed while the sister-in-law held the candle again glancing at the window where the daylight was growing. With my left hand steering the child's head, I used my ungloved right hand outside on her bare abdomen to press upon the fundus. The woman and I then got to work. Her two hands grabbed me at first a little timidly about the right wrist and forearm. Go ahead, I said. Pull hard. I welcomed the feel of her hands and the strong pull. It quieted me in the way the whole house had quieted me all night.

This woman in her present condition would have seemed repulsive to me ten years ago—now, poor soul, I see her to be as clean as a cow that calves. The flesh of my arm lay against the flesh of her knee gratefully. It was I who was being comforted and soothed.

Finally the head began to move. I wasn't sorry, thinking perhaps I'd have to do something radical before long. We kept at it till the head was born and I could leave her for a moment to put on my other glove. It was almost light now. What time is it? I asked the other woman. Six o'clock, she said.

Just after I had tied the cord, cut it and lifted the baby, a girl, to hand it to the woman, I saw the mother clutch herself suddenly between her thighs and give a cry. I was startled.

The other woman turned with a flash and shouted, Get out of here, you damned kids! I'll slap your damned face for you. And the door through which a head had peered was pulled closed. The three-year-old on the bed beside the mother stirred when the baby cried at first shrilly but had not wakened.

Oh yes, the drops in the baby's eyes. No need. She's as clean as a beast. How do I know? Medical discipline says every case must have drops in the eyes. No chance of gonorrhoea though here—but—Do it.

I heard her husband come into the kitchen now so we gave him the afterbirth in a newspaper to bury. Keep them damned kids out of here, his sister told him. Lock that door. Of course, there was no lock on it.

How do you feel now? I asked the mother after everything had been cleaned up. All right, she said with the peculiar turn of her head and smile by which I knew her.

How many is that? I asked the other woman. Five boys and three girls, she said. I've forgotten how to fix a baby, she went on. What shall I do? Put a little boric acid powder on the belly button to help dry it up?

Jean Beicke

DURING A TIME like this, they kid a lot among the doctors and nurses on the obstetrical floor because of the rushing business in new babies that's pretty nearly always going on up there. It's the Depression, they say, nobody has any money so they stay home nights. But one bad result of this is that in the children's ward, another floor up, you see a lot of unwanted children.

The parents get them into the place under all sorts of pretexts. For instance, we have two premature brats, Navarro and Cryschka, one a boy and one a girl; the mother died when Cryschka was born, I think. We got them within a few days of each other, one weighing four pounds and one a few ounces more. They dropped down below four pounds before we got them going but there they are; we had a lot of fun betting on their daily gains in weight but we still have them. They're in pretty good shape though now. Most of the kids that are left that way get along swell. The nurses grow attached to them and get a real thrill when they begin to pick up. It's great to see. And the parents sometimes don't even come to visit them, afraid we'll grab them and make them take the kids out, I suppose.

A funny one is a little Hungarian Gypsy girl that's been up there for the past month. She was about eight weeks old maybe when they brought her in with something on her lower lip that looked like a chancre. Everyone was interested but the Wassermann was negative. It turned out finally to be nothing but a peculiarly situated birthmark. But that kid is

69

still there too. Nobody can find the parents. Maybe they'll turn up some day.

Even when we do get rid of them, they often come back in a week or so—sometimes in terrible condition, full of impetigo, down in weight—everything we'd done for them to do over again. I think it's deliberate neglect in most cases. That's what happened to this little Gypsy. The nurse was funny after the mother had left the second time. I couldn't speak to her, she said. I just couldn't say a word I was so mad. I wanted to slap her.

We had a couple of Irish girls a while back named Cowley. One was a red head with beautiful wavy hair and the other a straight haired blonde. They really were good looking and not infants at all. I should say they must have been two and three years old approximately. I can't imagine how the parents could have abandoned them. But they did. I think they were habitual drunkards and may have had to beat it besides on short notice. No fault of theirs maybe.

But all these are, after all, not the kind of kids I have in mind. The ones I mean are those they bring in stinking dirty, and I mean stinking. The poor brats are almost dead sometimes, just living skeletons, almost, wrapped in rags, their heads caked with dirt, their eyes stuck together with pus and their legs all excoriated from the dirty diapers no one has had the interest to take off them regularly. One poor little pot we have now with a thin purplish skin and big veins standing out all over its head had a big sore place in the fold of its neck under the chin. The nurse told me that when she started to undress it it had on a shirt with a neckband that rubbed right into that place. Just dirt. The mother gave a story of having had it in some sort of home in Paterson. We couldn't get it straight. We never try. What the hell? We take 'em and try to make something out of them.

Sometimes, you'd be surprised, some doctor has given the parents a ride before they bring the child to the clinic. You wouldn't believe it. They clean 'em out, maybe for twenty-five dollars—they maybe had to borrow—and then tell 'em to move on. It happens. Men we all know too. Pretty bad. But what can you do?

And sometimes the kids are not only dirty and neglected but sick, ready to die. You ought to see those nurses work. You'd think it was the brat of their best friend. They handle those kids as if they were worth a million dollars. Not that some nurses aren't better than others but in general they break their hearts over those kids, many times, when I, for one, wish they'd never get well.

I often kid the girls. Why not? I look at some miserable specimens they've dolled up for me when I make the rounds in the morning and I tell them: Give it an enema, maybe it will get well and grow up into a cheap prostitute or something. The country needs you, brat. I once proposed that we have a mock wedding between a born garbage hustler we'd saved and a little female with a fresh mug on her that would make anybody smile.

Poor kids! You really wonder sometimes if medicine isn't all wrong to try to do anything for them at all. You actually want to see them pass out, especially when they're deformed or—they're awful sometimes. Every one has rickets in an advanced form, scurvy too, flat chests, spindly arms and legs. They come in with pneumonia, a temperature of a hundred and six, maybe, and before you can do a thing, they're dead.

This little Jean Beicke was like that. She was about the worst you'd expect to find anywhere. Eleven months old. Lying on the examining table with a blanket half way up her body, stripped, lying there, you'd think it a five months baby, just about that long. But when the nurse took the blanket away, her legs kept on going for a good eight inches longer. I couldn't get used to it. I covered her up and asked two of the men to guess how long she was. Both guessed at least half a foot too short. One thing that helped the illusion besides her small face was her arms. They came about to her hips. I don't know what made that. They should come down to her thighs, you know.

She was just skin and bones but her eyes were good and she looked straight at you. Only if you touched her any-where, she started to whine and then cry with a shrieking, distressing sort of cry that no one wanted to hear. We handled her as gently as we knew how but she had to cry just the same.

She was one of the damnedest looking kids I've ever seen. Her head was all up in front and flat behind, I suppose from lying on the back of her head so long the weight of it and the softness of the bones from the rickets had just flattened it out and pushed it up forward. And her legs and arms seemed loose on her like the arms and legs of some cheap dolls. You could bend her feet up on her shins absolutely flat—but there was no real deformity, just all loosened up. Nobody was with her when I saw her though her mother had brought her in.

It was about ten in the evening, the interne had asked me to see her because she had a stiff neck, and how! and there was some thought of meningitis—perhaps infantile paralysis. Anyhow, they didn't want her to go through the night with-out at least a lumbar puncture if she needed it. She had a fierce cough and a fairly high fever. I made it out to be a case of broncho-pneumonia with meningismus but no true involvement of the central nervous system. Besides she had inflamed ear drums.

I wanted to incise the drums, especially the left, and would have done it only the night superintendent came along just then and made me call the ear man on service. You know. She also looked to see if we had an operative release from the parents. There was. So I went home, the ear man came in a while later and opened the ears—a little bloody serum from both sides and that was that.

Next day we did a lumbar puncture, tapped the spine

that is, and found clear fluid with a few lymphocytes in it, nothing diagnostic. The X-ray of the chest clinched the diagnosis of broncho-pneumonia, there was an extensive involvement. She was pretty sick. We all expected her to die from exhaustion before she'd gone very far.

I had to laugh every time I looked at the brat after that, she was such a funny looking one but one thing that kept her from being a total loss was that she did eat. Boy! how that kid could eat! As sick as she was she took her grub right on time every three hours, a big eight ounce bottle of whole milk and digested it perfectly. In this depression you got to be such a hungry baby, I heard the nurse say to her once. It's a sign of intelligence, I told her. But anyway, we all got to be crazy about Jean. She'd just lie there and eat and sleep. Or she'd lie and look straight in front of her by the hour. Her eyes were blue, a pale sort of blue. But if you went to touch her, she'd begin to scream. We just didn't, that's all, unless we absolutely had to. And she began to gain in weight. Can you imagine that? I suppose she had been so terribly run down that food, real food, was an entirely new experience to her. Anyway she took her food and gained on it though her temperature continued to run steadily around between a hundred and three and a hundred and four for the first eight or ten days. We were surprised.

When we were expecting her to begin to show improvement, however, she didn't. We did another lumbar puncture and found fewer cells. That was fine and the second X-ray of the chest showed it somewhat improved also. That wasn't so good though, because the temperature still kept up and we had no way to account for it. I looked at the ears again and thought they ought to be opened once more. The ear man disagreed but I kept after him and next day he did it to please me. He didn't get anything but a drop of serum on either side.

Well, Jean didn't get well. We did everything we knew how to do except the right thing. She carried on for another

two—no I think it was three—weeks longer. A couple of
times her temperature shot up to a hundred and eight. Of
course we knew then it was the end. We went over her six
or eight times, three or four of us, one after the other, and
nobody thought to take an X-ray of the mastoid regions.
It was dumb, if you want to say it, but there wasn't a sign
of anything but the history of the case to point to it. The
ears had been opened early, they had been watched carefully, there was no discharge to speak of at any time and
from the external examination, the mastoid processes showed
no change from the normal. But that's what she died of,
acute purulent mastoiditis of the left side, going on to involvement of the left lateral sinus and finally the meninges.
We might, however, have taken a culture of the pus when
the ear was first opened and I shall always, after this, in
suspicious cases. I have been told since that if you get a
virulent bug like the streptococcus mucosus capsulatus it's
wise at least to go in behind the ear for drainage if the
temperature keeps up. Anyhow she died.

I went in when she was just lying there gasping. Somehow or other, I hated to see that kid go. Everybody felt
rotten. She was such a scrawny, misshapen, worthless piece
of humanity that I had said many times that somebody
ought to chuck her in the garbage chute—but after a month
watching her suck up her milk and thrive on it—and to see
those alert blue eyes in that face—well, it wasn't pleasant.
Her mother was sitting by the bed crying quietly when I
came in, the morning of the last day. She was a young
woman, didn't look more than a girl, she just sat there looking at the child and crying without a sound.

I expected her to begin to ask me questions with that
look on her face all doctors hate—but she didn't. I put my
hand on her shoulder and told her we had done everything
we knew how to do for Jean but that we really didn't
know what, finally, was killing her. The woman didn't
make any sign of hearing me. Just sat there looking in be-

tween the bars of the crib. So after a moment watching the poor kid beside her, I turned to the infant in the next crib to go on with my rounds. There was an older woman there looking in at that baby also—no better off than Jean, surely. I spoke to her, thinking she was the mother of this one, but she wasn't.

Before I could say anything, she told me she was the older sister of Jean's mother and that she knew that Jean was dying and that it was a good thing. That gave me an idea—I hated to talk to Jean's mother herself—so I beckoned the woman to come out into the hall with me.

I'm glad she's going to die, she said. She's got two others home, older, and her husband has run off with another woman. It's better off dead—never was any good anyway. You know her husband came down from Canada about a year and a half ago. She seen him and asked him to come back and live with her and the children. He come back just long enough to get her pregnant with this one then he left her again and went back to the other woman. And I suppose knowing she was pregnant, and suffering, and having no money and nowhere to get it, she was worrying and this one never was formed right. I seen it as soon as it was born. I guess the condition she was in was the cause. She's got enough to worry about now without this one. The husband's gone to Canada again and we can't get a thing out of him. I been keeping them, but we can't do much more. She'd work if she could find anything but what can you do with three kids in times like this? She's got a boy nine years old but her mother-in-law sneaked it away from her and now he's with his father in Canada. She worries about him too, but that don't do no good.

Listen, I said, I want to ask you something. Do you think she'd let us do an autopsy on Jean if she dies? I hate to speak to her of such a thing now but to tell you the truth, we've worked hard on that poor child and we don't exactly know what is the trouble. We know that she's had pneumonia but that's been getting well. Would you take it up with her for me, if—of course—she dies.

Oh, she's gonna die all right, said the woman. Sure, I will. If you can learn anything, it's only right. I'll see that you get the chance. She won't make any kick, I'll tell her.

Thanks, I said.

The infant died about five in the afternoon. The pathologist was dog-tired from a lot of extra work he'd had to do due to the absence of his assistant on her vacation so he put off the autopsy till next morning. They packed the body in ice in one of the service hoppers. It worked perfectly.

Next morning they did the postmortem. I couldn't get the nurse to go down to it. I may be a sap, she said, but I can't do it, that's all. I can't. Not when I've taken care of them. I feel as if they're my own.

I was amazed to see how completely the lungs had cleared up. They were almost normal except for a very small patch of residual pneumonia here and there which really amounted to nothing. Chest and abdomen were in excellent shape, otherwise, throughout—not a thing aside from the negligible pneumonia. Then he opened the head.

It seemed to me the poor kid's convolutions were unusually well developed. I kept thinking it's incredible that that complicated mechanism of the brain has come into being just for this. I never can quite get used to an autopsy.

The first evidence of the real trouble—for there had been no gross evidence of meningitis—was when the pathologist took the brain in his hand and made the long steady cut which opened up the left lateral ventricle. There was just a faint color of pus on the bulb of the choroid plexus there. Then the diagnosis all cleared up quickly. The left lateral sinus was completely thrombosed and on going into the left temporal bone from the inside the mastoid process was all broken down.

I called up the ear man and he came down at once. A clear miss, he said. I think if we'd gone in there earlier, we'd have saved her.

For what? said I. Vote the straight Communist ticket.

Would it make us any dumber? said the ear man.

A Face of Stone

HE WAS one of these fresh Jewish types you want to kill at sight, the presuming poor whose looks change the minute cash is mentioned. But they're insistent, trying to force attention, taking advantage of good nature at the first crack. You come when I call you, that type. He got me into a bad mood before he opened his mouth just by the half smiling, half insolent look in his eyes, a small, stoutish individual in a greasy black suit, a man in his middle twenties I should imagine.

She, on the other hand looked Italian, a goaty slant to her eyes, a face often seen among Italian immigrants. She had a small baby tight in her arms. She stood beside her smiling husband and looked at me with no expression at all on her pointed face, unless no expression is an expression. A face of stone. It was an animal distrust, not shyness. She wasn't shy but seemed as if sensing danger, as though she were on her guard against it. She looked dirty. So did he. Her hands were definitely grimy, with black nails. And she smelled, that usual smell of sweat and dirt you find among any people who habitually do not wash or bathe.

The infant was asleep when they came into the office, a child of about five months perhaps, not more.

People like that belong in clinics, I thought to myself. I wasn't putting myself out for them, not that day anyhow. Just dumb oxen. Why the hell do they let them into the country. Half idiots at best. Look at them.

My brother told us to bring the baby here, the man said. We've had a doctor but he's no good.

How do you know he's no good. You probably never gave him a chance. Did you pay him?

Sure we paid him.

Well what do you want me to do? To hell with you, I thought to myself. Get sore and get the hell out of here. I got to go home to lunch.

I want you to fix up the baby, Doc. My brother says you're the best baby doctor around here. And this kid's sick.

Well, put it up there on the table and take its clothes off then. Why didn't you come earlier instead of waiting here till the end of the hour. I got to live too.

The man turned to his wife. Gimme the baby, he said.

No. She wouldn't. Her face just took on an even stupider expression of obstinacy but she clung to the child.

Come on, come on, I said. I can't wait here all day.

Give him to me, he said to her again. He only wants to examine it.

I hold her, the woman said keeping the child firmly in her arms.

Listen here, I spoke to her. Do you want me to examine the child or don't you. If you don't, then take it somewhere.

Wait a minute, wait a minute, Doc, the man said smiling ingratiatingly.

You look at throat, the mother suggested.

You put the baby up there on the table and take its clothes off, I told her. The woman shook her head. But as she did so she gradually relented, looking furtively at me with distrustful glances her nostrils moving slightly.

Now what is it.

She's getting thin, Doc 'think somethink's the matter with her.

What do you mean, thin?

I asked her age, the kind of labor she had had. How they were feeding the baby. Vomiting, sleeping, hunger. It was the first child and the mother was new at nursing it. It was

four and a half months old and weighed thirteen and a
half pounds. Not bad.

I think my milk no good, said the woman, still clinging to
the baby whose clothes she had only begun to open.

As I approached them the infant took one look at me and
let out a wild scream. In alarm the mother clutched it to her
breast and started for the door.

I burst out laughing. The husband got red in the face but
forced a smile. Don't be so scared, he said to his wife. He,
nodding toward me, ain't gonna hurt you. You know she
hasn't been in this country long, Doc. She's scared you're
gonna hurt the baby. Bring it over here, he said to her and
take off his clothes. Here, give 'im to me. And he took the
infant into his own hands, screaming lustily, and carried it
to the table to undress it. The mother, in an agony of apprehension kept interfering from behind at every move.

What a time! I couldn't find much the matter and told
them so. Just the results of irregular, foolish routine and
probably insufficient breast milk. I gave them a complemen-
tal formula. He chiseled a dollar off the fee and—just as he
was going out—said, Doc, if we need you any time I want
you to come out to the house to see it. You gotta watch this
kid.

Where do you live, I asked.

He told me where it was, way out near the dumps. I'll
come if you give me a decent warning, I told him. If you
want me call me in the morning. Now get that. You can't
expect me to go running out there for nothing every time
the kid gets a belly ache. Or just because she thinks it's
dying. If you call me around supper time or in the middle of
a snow storm or at two o'clock in the morning maybe I
won't do it. I'm telling you now so you'll know. I got too
much to do already.

O.K., Doc, he said smiling. But you come.

I'll come on those conditions.

O.K., Doc.

And sure enough, on a Sunday night, about nine o'clock, with the thermometer at six below and the roads like a skating rink, they would call me.

Nothing doing, I said.

But Doc, you said you'd come.

I'm not going there tonight, I insisted. I won't do it. I'll ask my associate to make the call or some good younger man that lives in that neighborhood but I won't go over there tonight.

But we need you Doc, the baby's very sick.

Can't help it. I tell you I'm not going. And I slammed up the receiver.

Who in the world are you talking to like that, said my wife who had put down her book as my voice rose higher. You mustn't do that.

Leave me alone, I know what I'm doing.

But my dear!

Four months later, after three months of miserable practice, the first warm day in April, about twenty women with babies came to my office. I started at one P.M. and by three I was still going strong. I hadn't loafed. Anybody left out there? I asked the last woman, as I thought, who had been waiting for me. Oh yes, there's a couple with a baby. Oh Lord, I groaned. It was half past three by then and a number of calls still to be made about the town.

There they were. The same fresh mug and the same face of stone, still holding the baby which had grown, however,. to twice its former size.

Hello Doc, said the man smiling.

For a moment I couldn't place them. Hello, I said. Then I remembered. What can I do for you—at this time of day. Make it snappy cause I've got to get out.

Just want you to look the baby over, Doc.

Oh yeah.

Listen Doc, we've been waiting out there two hours.

Good night! That finishes me for the afternoon, I said to

myself. All right, put it up on the table. As I said this, feeling at the same time a sense of helpless irritation and anger, I noticed a cluster of red pimples in the region of the man's right eyebrow and reaching to the bridge of his nose. Like bed-bug bites I thought to myself. He'll want me to do something for them too before I get through I suppose. Well, what's the matter now? I asked them.

It's the baby again, Doc, the man said.

What's the matter with the baby. It looks all right to me. And it did. A child of about ten months, I estimated, with a perfectly happy, round face.

Yes, but his body isn't so good.

I want you should examine him all over, said the mother.

You would, I said. Do you realize what time it is?

Shall she take his clothes off? the man broke in.

Suit yourself, I answered, hoping she wouldn't do it. But she put the infant on the table and began carefully to undress it.

No use. I sat down and took out a card for the usual notes. How old is it?

How old is it? he asked his wife.

Ten months. Next Tuesday ten months, she said with the same face on her as always.

Are you still nursing it.

Sure, she said. Him won't take bottle.

Do you mean to say that after what I told you last time, you haven't weaned the baby?

What can she do, Doc. She tried to but he won't let go of the breast. You can't make him take a bottle.

Does he eat?

Yeah, he eats a little, but he won't take much.

Cod liver oil?

He takes it all right but spits it up half an hour later. She stopped giving it to him.

Orange juice.

Sure. Most of the time.

So, as a matter of fact, she's been nursing him and giving him a little cereal and that's all.

Sure, that's about right.

How often does she nurse him?

Whenever he wants it, the man grinned. Sometimes every two hours. Sometimes he sleeps. Like that.

But didn't I tell you, didn't I tell her to feed it regularly.

She can't do that, Doc. The baby cries and she gives it to him.

Why don't you put it in a crib?

She won't give it up. You know, that's the way she is, Doc. You can't make her do different. She wants the baby next to her so she can feel it.

Have you got it undressed? I turned to the mother who was standing with her back to me.

You want shoe off? she answered me.

Getting up I went to the infant and pulled the shoes and stockings off together, picked the thing up by its feet and the back of the neck and carried it to the scales. She was right after me, her arms half extended watching the child at every movement I made. Fortunately the child grinned and sagged back unresisting in my grasp. I looked at it more carefully then, a smart looking little thing and a perfectly happy, fresh mug on him that amused me in spite of myself.

Twenty pounds and four ounces, I said. What do you want for a ten month old baby? There's nothing the matter with him. Get his clothes on.

I want you should examine him first, said the mother.

The blood went to my face in anger but she paid no attention to me. He too thin, she said. Look him body.

To quiet my nerves I took my stethoscope and went rapidly over the child's chest, saw that everything was all right there, that there was no rickets and told them so— and to step on it. Get him dressed. I got to get out of here.

Him all right? the woman questioned me with her stony

pale green eyes. I stopped to look at them, they were very curious, almost at right angles to each other—in a way of speaking—like the eyes of some female figure I had seen somewhere—Mantegna—Botticelli—I couldn't remember.

Yes, only for God's sake, take him off the breast. Feed him the way I told you to.

No will take bottle.

Fine. I don't give a damn about the bottle. Feed him from a cup, with a spoon, anyway at all. But feed him regularly. That's all.

As I turned to wash my hands, preparatory to leaving the office the man stopped me. Doc, he said, I want you to examine my wife.

He got red in the face as I turned on him. What the hell do you think I am anyhow. You got a hell of a nerve. Don't you know . . .

We waited two hours and ten minutes for you, Doc, he replied smiling. Just look her over and see what the matter with her is.

I could hardly trust myself to speak for a moment but, instead turned to look at her again standing beside the baby which she had finished dressing and which was sitting on the table looking at me. What a creature. What a face. And what a body. I looked her coldly up and down from head to toe. There was a rip in her dress, a triangular tear just above the left knee.

Well— No use getting excited with people such as these— or with anyone, for that matter, I said in despair. No one can do two things at the same time, especially when they're in two different places. I simply gave up and returned to my desk chair.

Go ahead. What's the matter with her?

She gets pains in her legs, especially at night. And she's got a spot near her right knee. It came last week, a big blue looking sort of spot.

Did she ever have rheumatism? You know, go to bed with swollen joints—for six weeks—or like that.

She simply shrugged her shoulders.

Did you have rheumatism? he turned to her.

She don't know, he said, interpreting and turning red in the face again. I particularly noticed it this time and remembered that it had occurred two or three times before while we were talking.

Tell her to open up her dress.

Open up your dress, he said.

Sit down, I told her and let me see your legs.

As she did so I noticed again the triangular rip in the skirt over her left thigh, dirty silk, and that her skin was directly under it. She untied some white rags above her knees and let down her black stockings. The left one first, I said.

Her lower legs were peculiarly bowed, really like Turkish scimitars, flattened and somewhat rotated on themselves in an odd way that could not have come from anything but severe rickets rather late in her childhood. The whole leg while not exactly weak was as ugly and misshapen as a useful leg well could be in so young a woman. Near the knee was a large discolored area where in all probability a varicose vein had ruptured.

That spot, I told her husband, comes from a broken varicose vein.

Yeah, I thought so, she's got them all up both legs.

That's from carrying a child.

No. She had them before that. They've always been that way since I've known her. Is that what makes her have the pains there?

I hardly think so, I said looking over the legs again, one of which I held on the palm of either hand. No, I don't think so.

What is it then? It hurts her bad, especially at night.

She's bow-legged as hell in the first place. That throws the strain where it doesn't belong and look at these shoes—

Yeah, I know.

The woman had on an old pair of fancy high-heeled slippers such as a woman might put on for evening wear. They were all worn and incredibly broken down. I don't see how she can walk in them.

That's what I told her, the man said. I wanted her to get a pair of shoes that fitted her but she wouldn't do it.

Well, she's got to do it, I said. Throw away those shoes, I told her, and get shoes with flat heels. And straight heels. I tried to impress her. What they call Cuban heels, if you must. New shoes, I emphasized. How old is she, I asked the man.

His face colored again for reasons I could not fathom. Twenty-four, he said.

Where was she born?

In Poland.

In Poland! Well. I looked at her, not believing him.

Yeah, why?

Well. Twenty-four years old you say. Let's see. That's different. An unusual type for a Jew, I thought. That's the probable explanation for her legs, I told the husband. She must have been a little girl during the war over there. A kid of maybe five or six years I should imagine. Is that right, I asked her. But she didn't answer me, just looked back into my eyes with that inane look.

What did you get to eat?

She seemed not to have heard me but turned to her husband.

Did she lose any of her people, I asked him.

Any of them? She lost everybody, he said quietly.

How did she come to get over here then?

She came over four years ago. She has a sister over here.

So that's it, I thought to myself looking at her fussing, intensely absorbed with the baby, looking at it, talking to it in an inarticulate sort of way, paying no attention whatever to me. No wonder she's built the way she is, considering what she must have been through in that invaded territory. And this guy here—

What are we going to do about the pains, Doc?

Get her some decent shoes, that's the first thing.

O.K., Doc.

She could be operated on for those veins. But I wouldn't advise it, just yet. I tell you. Get one of those woven elastic bandages for her, they don't cost much. A three inch one. And I told him what to get.

Can't you give her some pills to stop the pain?

Not me, I told him. You might get her teeth looked at though if you want to. All that kind of thing and—well, I will give you something. It's not dope. It just helps if there's any rheumatism connected with it.

Can you swallow a pill, I turned to her attracting her attention.

She looked at me. How big? she said.

She swallows an Aspirin pill when I give it to her sometimes, said her husband, but she usually puts it in a spoonful of water first to dissolve it. His face reddened again and suddenly I understood his half shameful love for the woman and at the same time the extent of her reliance on him.

I was touched.

They're pretty big pills, I said. Look, they're green. That's the coating so they won't dissolve in your stomach and upset your digestion.

Let see, said the woman.

I showed a few of the pills to her in the palm of my hand.

For pains in leg?

Yes, I told her.

She looked at them again. Then for the first time since I had known her a broad smile spread all over her face. Yeah, she said, I swallow him.

Danse Pseudomacabre

THAT WHICH IS POSSIBLE is inevitable. I defend the normality of every distortion to which the flesh is susceptible, every disease, every amputation. I challenge anyone who thinks to discomfit my intelligence by limiting the import of what I say to the expounding of a shallow morbidity, to prove that health alone is inevitable. Until he can do that his attack upon me will be imbecilic.

Allons! Commençons la danse.

The telephone is ringing. I have awakened sitting erect in bed, unsurprised, almost uninterested, but with an overwhelming sense of death pressing my chest together as if I had come reluctant from the grave to which a distorted homesickness continued to drag me, a sense as of the end of everything. My wife lies asleep, curled against her pillow. Christ, Christ! how can I ever bear to be separated from this my boon companion, to be annihilated, to have her annihilated? How can a man live in the face of this daily uncertainty? How can a man not go mad with grief, with apprehension?

I wonder what time it is. There is a taxi just leaving the club. Tang, tang, tang. Finality. Three o'clock.

The moon is low, its silent flame almost level among the trees, across the budding rose garden, upon the grass.

The streets are illumined with the moon and the useless flares of the purple and yellow street lamps hanging from the dark each above its little circular garden of flowers.

Hurry, hurry, hurry! Upstairs! He's dying! Oh my God!

my God, what will I do without him? I won't live! I won't
—I won't—

What a face! Erysipelas. Doesn't look so bad—in a few
days the moon will be full.

Quick! Witness this signature— It's his will— A great
blubber of a thirty-year-old male seated, hanging, floating
erect in the center of the sagging double-bed spring, his
long hair in a mild mass, his body wrapped in a downy
brown wool dressing gown, a cord around the belly, a great
pudding face, the whole right side of it a dirty purple,
swollen, covered with watery blebs, the right eye swollen
shut. He is trembling, wildly excited—a paper on his un-
steady knees, a fountain pen in his hand. Witness this signature! Will it be legal? Yes, of course. He signs. I sign after
him. When the Scotch go crazy they are worse than a Latin.
The nose uninvolved. What a small nose.

My God, I'm done for.

Oh my God, what will I do without him?

Kindly be quiet, madam. What sort of way is that to
talk in a sickroom? Do you want to kill him? Give him a
chance, if you please.

Is he going to die, doctor? He's only been sick a few days.
His eye started to close yesterday. He's never been sick in
his life. He has no one but his father and me. Oh, I won't
live without him.

Of course when a man as full-blooded as he is has erysipelas—

Do you think it's erysipelas?

How much does he weigh?

Two hundred and forty pounds.

Temperature 102. That's not bad.

He won't die? Are you kidding me, doctor?

What for? The moon has sunk. Almost no more at all.
Only the Scotch have such small noses. Follow these directions. I have written down what you are to do.

Again the moon. Again. And why not again? It is a

dance. Everything that varies a hair's breadth from another is an invitation to the dance. Either dance or annihilation. There can be only the dance or ONE. So, the next night, I enter another house. And so I repeat the trouble of writing that which I have already written, and so drag another human being from oblivion to serve my music.

It is a baby. There is a light at the end of a broken corridor. A man in a pointed beard leads the way. Strong foreign accent. Holland Dutch. We walk through the corridor to the back of the house. The kitchen. In the kitchen turn to the right. Someone is sitting back of the bedroom door. A nose, an eye emerge, sniffing and staring, a wrinkled nose, a cavernous eye. Turn again to the right through another door and walk toward the front of the house. We are in a sickroom. A bed has been backed against the corridor entry making this detour necessary.

Oh, here you are, doctor. British. The nurse I suppose.

The baby is in a smother of sheets and crumpled blankets, its head on a pillow. The child's left eye closed, its right partly opened. It emits a soft whining cry continuously at every breath. It can't be more than a few weeks old.

Do you think it is unconscious, doctor?

Yes.

Will it live? It is the mother. A great tender-eyed blonde. Great full breasts. A soft gentle-minded woman of no mean beauty. A blue cotton house wrapper, shoulder to ankle.

If it lives it will be an idiot perhaps. Or it will be paralysed—or both. It is better for it to die.

There it goes now! The whining has stopped. The lips are blue. The mouth puckers as for some diabolic kiss. It twitches, twitches faster and faster, up and down. The body slowly grows rigid and begins to fold itself like a flower folding again. The left eye opens slowly, the eyeball is turned so the pupil is lost in the angle of the nose. The right eye remains open and fixed staring forward. Meningitis. Acute. The arms are slowly raised more and more from the sides as if in the deliberate attitude before a mad dance, hands clenched, wrists flexed. The arms now lie upon each other crossed at the wrists. The knees are drawn up as if the child were squatting. The body holds this posture, the child's belly rumbling with a huge contortion. Breath has stopped. The body is stiff, blue. Slowly it relaxes, the whimpering cry begins again. The left eye falls closed.

It began with that eye. It was a lovely baby. Normal in every way. Breast fed. I have not taken it anywhere. It is only six weeks old. How can he get it?

The pointed beard approaches. It is infection, is it not, doctor?

Yes.

But I took him nowhere. How could he get it?

He must have gotten it from someone who carries it, maybe from one of you.

Will he die?

Yes, I think so.

Oh, I pray God to take him.

Have you any other children?

One girl five, and this boy.

Well, one must wait.

Again the night. The beard has followed me to the door. He closes the door carefully. We are alone in the night.

It is an infection?

Yes.

My wife is Catholic—not I. She had him for baptism. They pour water from a can on his head, so. It runs down in front of him, there where they baptize all kinds of babies, into his eye perhaps. It is a funny thing.

The Paid Nurse

WHEN I CAME IN, approaching eleven o'clock Sunday evening, there had been a phone call for me. I don't know what it is, Mrs. Corcoran called up, said Floss, about an accident of some sort that happened to George. You know, Andy's friend. What kind of an accident? An explosion, I don't know, something like that, I couldn't make it out. He wants to come up and see you. She'll call back in a minute or two.

As I sat down to finish the morning paper the phone rang again as usual. His girl friend had heard about it and was taking him up to her doctor in Norwood. Swell.

But next day he came to see me anyhow. What in hell's happened to you, George? I said when I saw him. His right arm was bandaged to the shoulder, the crook of his left elbow looked like overdone bacon, his lips were blistered, his nose was shiny with grease and swollen out of shape and his right ear was red and thickened.

They want me to go back to work, he said. They told me if I didn't go back I wouldn't get paid. I want to see you.

What happened?

I work for the General Bearings Company, in Jersey City. You know what that means. They're a hard-boiled outfit. I'm not kidding myself about that, but they can't make me work the way I feel. Do you think I have to work with my arms like this? I want your opinion. That fellow in Norwood said it wasn't anything but I couldn't sleep last night. I was in agony. He gave me two capsules and told me to take one. I took one around three o'clock and that just made me feel worse. I tried to go back this morning but I couldn't do it.

Wait a minute, wait a minute. You haven't told me what happened yet.

Well, they had me cleaning some metal discs. It wasn't my regular job. So I asked the boss, What is this stuff? Benzol, he said. It is inflammable? I said. Not very, he said. We use it here all the time. I didn't believe him right then because I could smell it, it had a kind of smell like gasoline or cleaning fluid of some kind.

What I had to do was to pick those pieces out of a pail of the stuff on this side of me, my left side, and turn and place them in the oven to dry them. Two hundred degrees temperature in there. Then I'd turn and pick up another lot and so on into the dryer and back again. I had on long rubber gauntlets up almost to my elbow.

Well, I hadn't hardly started when, blup! it happened. I didn't know what it was at first. You know you don't realize those things right away—until I smelt burnt hair and cloth and saw my gloves blazing. The front of my shirt was burning too—lucky it wasn't soaked with the stuff. I jumped back into the aisle and put my hands back of me and shook the gloves off on the floor. The pail was blazing too.

Everybody came on the run and rushed me into the emergency room. Everybody was excited, but as soon as they saw that I could see and wasn't going to pass out on them they went back to their jobs and left me there with the nurse to fix me up.

Then I began to feel it. The flames from the shirt must have come up into my face because inside my nostrils was burnt and you can see what it did to my eyebrows and eyelashes. She called the doctor but he didn't come any nearer than six feet from me. That's not very bad, he said. So the nurse put a little dressing, of tannic acid, I think she said it was, on my right arm which got the worst of it. I was just turning away from the oven when it happened, lucky for me, so I got it mostly on my right side.

What do I do now? I asked her. Go home? I was feeling rotten.

No, of course not, she told me. That's not bad. Go on back to work.

What! I said.

Yes, she said. And come back tomorrow morning. If you don't you won't get paid. And, by the way, she said, don't go to any other doctor. You come back here tomorrow morning and go to work as usual. Do you think that was right?

The bastards. Go ahead. Wasn't there someone you could appeal to there? Don't you belong to a union?

No, said George. There's nothing like that there. Only the teamsters and the pressmen have unions, they've had them long enough so that the company can't interfere.

All right. Go ahead.

So I went back to the job. They gave me something else to do but the pain got so bad I couldn't stand it so I told the boss I had to quit. All right, he said, go on home but be back here tomorrow morning. That would be today.

You went back this morning?

I couldn't sleep all night. Look at my arm.

All right. Let's look at it. The worst was the right elbow and forearm, almost to the shoulder in fact. It was cooked to about the color of ham rind with several areas where the Norwood doctor had opened several large blisters the night before. The arm was, besides that, swollen to a size at least a third greater than its normal volume and had begun to turn a deep, purplish red just above the wrist. The ear and nose were not too bad but in all the boy looked sick.

So you went back this morning?

Yes.

Did they dress it?

No, just looked at it and ordered me on the floor. They gave me a job dragging forty-pound cases from the stack to the elevator. I couldn't use my right arm so I tried to do it with my left but I couldn't keep it up. I told 'em I was going home.

Well?

The nurse gave me hell. She called me a baby and told me it wasn't anything. The men work with worse things than that the matter with them every day, she said.

That don't make any difference to me, I told her, I'm going home.

All right, she said, but if you don't show up here tomorrow for work you don't get any pay. That's why I'm here, he continued. I can't work. What do you say?

Well, I said, I'll call up the Senator, which I did at once. And was told, of course, that the man didn't have to go to work if I said he wasn't able to do so. They can be reported to the Commission, if necessary. Or better perhaps, I can write them a letter first. You tell him not to go to work.

You're not to go to work, I told the boy. O.K., that settles it. Want to see me tomorrow? Yeah. And quit those damned capsules he gave you, I told him. No damned good. Here, here's something much simpler that won't at least leave you walking on your ear till noon the next day. Thanks. See you tomorrow.

Then it began to happen. Late in the afternoon the nurse called him up to remind him to report for duty next morning. I told her I'd been to you, he said, and that you wanted the compensation papers. She won't listen to it. She says they're sending the company car for me tomorrow morning to take me in to see their doctor. Do I go?

Not on your life.

But the next day I was making rounds in the hospital at about ten A.M. when the office reached me on one of the floors. Hold the wire. It was George. The car is here and they want me to go back with them. What do I do?

Wait a minute, I said. What's their phone number? And what's that nurse's name? I'll talk to them. You wait till I call you back. So I got the nurse and talked to her. I hear you had an explosion down at your plant, I told her. What do you mean? she said. What are you trying to do, cover it

up, I asked her, so the insurance company won't find out
about it? We don't do that sort of thing in this company.
What are you doing now? I asked her again. She blurted and
bubbled till I lost my temper and let her have it. What is
that, what is that? she kept saying. You know what I'm talking about, I told her. Our doctors take care of our own cases,
she told me. You mean they stand off six feet from a man
and tell him he's all right when the skin is half-burned off
of him and the insides of his nostrils are all scorched? That
isn't true, she said. He had no right to go to an outside
doctor. What! I said, when he's in agony in the middle of
the night from the pains of his burns, he has no right to get
advice and relief? Is that what you mean? He has the privilege of calling our own doctor if he needs one, she says. In
the middle of the night? I asked her. I tell you what you do,
I said, you send me the compensation papers to sign. You
heard me, I said, and make it snappy if you know what's
good for you. We want our own doctor to see him, she
insisted. All right, I said, your own doctor can see him but
he's not to go to work. Get that through your head, I said.
And that's what I told him.

He went back to their doctor in the company car.

It was funny. We were at supper that evening when he
came to the house door. I didn't have any office hours that
night. Floss asked him to come in and join us but he had
eaten. He had a strange look on his face, half-amused and
half-bewildered.

I don't know, he said. I couldn't believe it. You ought to
see the way I was treated. I was all ready to be bawled out
but, oh no! The nurse was all smiles. Come right in, George.
Do you feel all right, George? You don't look very well.
Don't you want to lie down here on the couch? I thought
she was kidding me. But she meant it. What a difference!
That isn't the way they treated me the first time. Then she
says, It's so hot in here I'll turn on the fan so as to cool you

a little. And here, here's a nice glass of orange juice. No kiddin'. What a difference!

Floss and I burst out laughing in spite of ourselves. Oh, everything's lovely now, he said. But you're not working? No, I don't have to work. They sent me back home in the company car and they're calling for me tomorrow morning. The only thing is they brought in the man who got me the job. That made me feel like two cents. You shouldn't have acted like that, George, he told me. We'll take care of you. We always take care of our men.

I can take it, sir, I told him. But I simply couldn't go back to work after the burning I got. You didn't have to go back to work, he said. Yes, I did, I said. They had me dragging forty-pound cases around the floor . . . .

Really? he said.

He didn't know that, did he? I interposed. I'm glad you spoke up. And they want you to go back tomorrow?

All right, but don't work till I tell you. But he did. After all, jobs aren't so easy to get nowadays even with a hard-boiled firm like that. I won't get any compensation either, they told me, not even for a scar.

Is that so?

And they said they're not going to pay you, either.

We'll see what the Senator says about that.

He came back two days later to tell me the rest of it. I get it now, he said. It seems after you've been there a year they insure you, but before that you don't get any protection. After a year one of the fellows was telling me—why, they had a man there that just sprained his ankle a little. It wasn't much. But they kept him out on full pay for five months, what do you know about that? They wouldn't let him work when he wanted to.

Good night!

Geez, it was funny today, he went on. They were dressing my arm and a big piece of skin had all worked loose and they were peeling it off. It hurt me a little, oh, you know, not much but I showed I could feel it, I guess. My God! the nurse had me lie down on the couch before I knew what she was doing. And do you know, that was around one-thirty. I didn't know what happened to me. When I woke up it was four o'clock. I'd been sleeping all that time! They had a blanket over me and everything.

Good!

How much do I owe you? Because I want to pay you. No use trying to get it from them. If I make any trouble they'll blackball me all over the country they tell me.

Ancient Gentility

In those days I was about the only doctor they would have on Guinea Hill. Nowadays some of the kids I delivered then may be practising medicine in the neighborhood. But in those days I had them all. I got to love those people, they were all right. Italian peasants from the region just south of Naples, most of them, living in small jerry-built houses— doing whatever they could find to do for a living and getting by, somehow.

Among the others, there was a little frame building, or box, you might almost say, which had always interested me but into which I had never gone. It stood in the center of the usual small garden patch and sometimes there would be an old man at the gate, just standing there, with a big curved and silver-capped pipe in his mouth, puffing away at his leisure.

Sure enough, one day I landed in that house also.

I had been seeing a child at the Petrello's or Albino's or whoever it was when, as often happened, the woman of the house stopped me with a smile at the door just as I was leaving.

Doc, I want you to visit the old people next door. The old lady's sick. She don't want to call nobody, but you go just the same. I'll fix it up with you sometime. Will you do it—for me?

Would I! It was a June morning. I had only to go twenty feet or so up the street—with a view of all New York City spread out before me over the meadows just beginning to turn green—and push back the low gate to the little vegetable garden.

The old man opened the house door for me before I

could knock. He smiled and bowed his head several times out of respect for a physician and pointed upstairs. He couldn't speak a word of English and I knew practically no Italian, so he let it go at that.

He was wonderful. A gentle, kindly creature, big as the house itself, almost, with long pure white hair and big white moustache. Every movement he made showed a sort of ancient gentility. Finally he said a few words as if to let me know he was sorry he couldn't talk English and pointed upstairs again.

Where I stood at that moment it was just one room, everything combined: you cooked in one corner, ate close by, and sat yourself down to talk with your friends and relatives over beyond. Everything was immaculately clean and smelt just tinged with that faint odor of garlic, peppers and olive oil which one gets to expect in all these peasant houses.

There was one other room, immediately above. To it there ascended a removable ladder. At this moment the trap was open and the ladder in place. I went up. The old man remained below.

What a thrill I got! There was an enormous bed that almost filled the place, it seemed, perhaps a chair or two besides, but no other furniture, and in the bed sinking into the feather mattress and covered with a great feather quilt was the woman I had been summoned to attend.

Her face was dry and seamed with wrinkles, as old peasant faces will finally become, but it had the same patient smile upon it as shone from that of her old husband. White hair framing her face with silvery abundance, she didn't look at all sick to me.

She said a few words, smiling the while, by which I understood that after all it wasn't much and that she knew she didn't need a doctor and would have been up long since—or words to that effect—if the others hadn't insisted. After listening to her heart and palpating her abdomen I told her she could get up if she wanted to, and as I backed down the ladder after saying good-bye, she had already begun to do so.

The old man was waiting for me as I arrived below.

We walked to the door together, I trying to explain to him what I had found and he bowing and saying a word or two of Italian in reply. I could make out that he was thanking me for my trouble and that he was sorry he had no money, and so forth and so on.

At the gate we paused in one of those embarrassed moments which sometimes arrive during any conversation between relative strangers who wish to make a good impression on each other. Then as we stood there, slightly ill at ease, I saw him reach into his vest pocket and take something into his hand which he held out toward me.

It was a small silver box, about an inch and a quarter along the sides and half an inch thick. On the cover of it was the embossed figure of a woman reclining among flowers. I took it in my hand but couldn't imagine what he wanted me to do with it. He couldn't be giving it to me?

Seeing that I was puzzled, he reached for it, ever so gently, and I returned it to him. As he took it in his hand he opened it. It seemed to contain a sort of brown powder. Then I saw him pick some of it up between the thumb and finger of his right hand, place it at the base of his left thumb and . . .

Why snuff! Of course. I was delighted.

As he whiffed the powder into one generous nostril and then the other, he handed the box back to me—in all, one of the most gracious, kindly proceedings I had ever taken part in.

Imitating him as best I could, I shared his snuff with him, and that was about the end of me for a moment or two. I couldn't stop sneezing. I suppose I had gone at it a little too vigorously. Finally, with tears in my eyes, I felt the old man standing there, smiling, an experience the like of which I shall never, in all probability, have again in my life on this mundane sphere.

Verbal Transcription—6 A. M.

ABOUT AN HOUR AGO. He woke up and it was as if a knife was sticking in his side. I tried the old reliable, I gave him a good drink of whisky but this time it did no good. I thought it might be his heart so I . . . Yes. In between his pains he was trying to get dressed. He could hardly stand up but through it all he was trying to get himself ready to go to work. Can you imagine that?

Rags! Leave the man alone. The minute you're good to him he . . . Look at him sitting up and begging! Rags! Come here! Do you want to look out of the window? Oh, yes. That's his favorite amusement—like the rest of the family. And we're not willing just to look out. We have to lean out as if we were living on Third Avenue.

Two dogs killed our old cat last week. He was thirteen years old. That's unusual for a cat, I think. We never let him come upstairs. You know he was stiff and funny looking. But we fed him and let him sleep in the cellar. He was deaf and I suppose he couldn't fight for himself and so they killed him.

Yes. We have quite a menagerie. Have you seen our blue-jay? He had a broken wing. We've had him two years now. He whistles and answers us when we call him. He doesn't look so good but he likes it here. We let him out of the cage sometimes with the window open. He goes to the sill and looks out. Then he turns and runs for his cage as if he was scared. Sometimes he sits on the little dog's head and they are great friends. If he went out I'm afraid he wouldn't understand and they would kill him too.

And a canary. Yes. You know I was afraid it was his heart. Shall I dress him now? This is the time he usually takes the train to be there at seven o'clock. Pajamas are so cold. Here put on this old shirt—this old horse blanket, I always call it. I'm sorry to be such a fool but those needles give me a funny feeling all over. I can't watch you give them. Thank you so much for coming so quickly. I have a cup of coffee for you all ready in the kitchen.

The Insane

WHAT ARE they teaching you now, son? said the old Doc brushing the crumbs from his vest.

Have one, Dad? Yeah. Throw it to me. I got matches.

I wish you wouldn't do that, said his wife trying hard to scowl. It was the usual Saturday evening dinner, the young man, a senior in medical school, out for his regular weekend siesta in the suburbs.

I'm curious, said the old Doc glancing at his wife. Then to his son, Anything new? She placed an ash tray at his elbow.

I go on Medicine Monday, said the boy. We finished Pediatrics and Psychiatry today.

Psychiatry, eh? That's one you won't regret, said his father. Or do you like it, maybe?

Not particularly. But what can we learn in a few weeks? The cases we get are so advanced, just poor dumb clucks, there's nothing to do for them anyway. I can see though that there must be a lot to it.

What are you two talking about? said his mother.

Insanity, Ma.

Oh.

Any new theories as to causes? said the older man. I mean, not the degenerative cases, with a somatic background, but the schizophrenics especially. Have they learned anything new about that in recent years?

Oh, Dad, there are all sorts of theories. It starts with birth in most cases, they tell us. Even before birth sometimes.

That's what we're taught. Unwanted children, conflicts of one sort or another. You know.

No. I'm curious. What do they tell you about Freud?

Sex as the basis for everything? The boy's mother looked up at him a moment and then down again.

It's largely a reflection of his own personality, most likely. I mean it's all right to look to sex as a cause, but that's just the surface aspect of the thing. Not the thing itself. Don't you think?

That's what I'm asking you.

But everybody has a different theory. One thing I can understand though, even from my little experience, and that is why insanity is increasing so rapidly here today.

Really? said his mother.

I mean from my Pediatric work. He paused. Of the twenty-five children I saw in the clinic this week only two can be said to be really free from psychoneurotic symptoms. Two! Out of twenty-five. And maybe a more careful history would have found something even in those two.

Do you mean that those children all showed signs of beginning insanity? said his mother.

Potentially, yes.

Not a very reassuring comment on modern life, is it?

Go ahead, son, said his father.

Take a funny-faced little nine-year-old guy with big glasses I saw in the clinic this afternoon. His mother brought him in for stealing money.

How old a child, did you say?

Nine years. The history was he'd take money from her purse. Or if she sent him to the store to buy something, he'd come back without it and use the money for something he wanted himself.

Do you have to treat those cases too? asked his mother.

Anything that comes in. We have to get the history, do a physical, a complete physical—you know what that means, Dad—make a diagnosis and prescribe treatment.

What did you find?

The story is this. The lad's father was a drunk who died two years ago when the boy was just seven. A typical drunk. The usual bust up. They took him to the hospital and he died.

But before that—to go back, this boy had been a caesarian birth. He has a brother, three years younger, an accident. After that the woman was sterilized. But I'll tell you about him later.

Anyhow, when she came home, on the ninth day after her caesarian, she found her husband under the influence, dead drunk as usual and he started to take her over—that's the story.

What's that?

Oh, you know, Mother. Naturally she put up a fight and as a result he knocked her downstairs.

What! Nine days after her confinement?

Yes, nine days after the section. She had to return to the hospital for a check up. And naturally when she came out again she hated her husband and the baby too because it was his child.

Terrible.

And the little chap had to grow up in that atmosphere. They were always battling. The old man beat up his wife regularly and the child had to witness it for his entire existence up to two years ago.

As I say, she had a second child—three years old now, which, though she hated it, came between the older boy and his mother forcing them apart still further. That one has tuberculosis which doesn't make things any easier.

Imagine such people!

They're all around you, Mother, if you only knew it. Oh, I forgot to tell you the older kid was the dead spit of his dad who had always showered all kinds of attentions on him. His favorite. All the love the kid ever knew came from his old man.

So when the father died the only person the boy could look to for continued affection was his mother—who hated him.

Oh, no!

As a result the child doesn't eat, has lost weight, doesn't sleep, constipation and all the rest of it. And in school, whereas his marks had always been good—because he's fairly bright—after his father died they went steadily down, down and down to complete failure.

Poor baby.

And then he began to steal—from his mother—because he couldn't get the love he demanded of her. He began to steal from her to compensate for what he could not get otherwise, and which his father had given him formerly.

Interesting. Isn't it, dear?

So young!

The child substitutes his own solution for the reality which he needs and cannot obtain. Unreality and reality become confused in him. Finally he loses track. He doesn't know one from the other and we call him insane.

What will become of him in this case? asked the mother.

In this case, said her son, the outcome is supposed to be quite favorable. We'll explain the mechanism to the woman —who by the way isn't in such good condition herself— and if she follows up what she's told to do the boy is likely to be cured.

Strange, isn't it? said the old Doc.

But what gets me, said his son. Of course we're checked up on all these cases; they're all gone over by a member of the staff. And when we give a history like that, they say, Oh those are just the psychiatric findings. That gripes me. Why, it's the child's life.

Good boy, said his father. You're all right. Stick to it.

Comedy Entombed: 1930

Yᴇᴀʜ, I know, I said. But I can't go three places first.

When can you come then? he answered.

I told you I've already promised two people to see them as soon as I've had breakfast. Why don't you get somebody nearer if you're in such a hurry?

Because I want you. You know where it is, don't you?

I'll find it.

There's a little wooden house behind the shoe shop between Fourth and Fifth. I'll be looking for you. You sure you'll come.

Oh, Lord! I said, hanging up the receiver. What next?

Did you get the name? said Floss.

No. Porphyrio, Principio—something like that.

Well, she answered me, shrugging her shoulders.

There he was, at ten sharp, waiting on the street, coatless, with a narrow face and his hair standing up long and straight at the top to make it seem still narrower.

I felt a little self-conscious as I got out of the car in my light-gray broadcloth suit and gray topcoat and went to follow him. The old car seemed large and costly in those poor surroundings, especially so before that diminutive wooden house. The place as if it had been abandoned long since and later reclaimed it was so tumble-down and yet attractive.

That old familiar smell—of greasy dirt—greeted me as we stepped inside the door. It was a pleasant October day and the stove wasn't on full so there was no emphasis, but there wasn't a clean place to lay my coat. I chose a green painted kitchen chair, folding the coat up into a little pudding so it wouldn't spread over too much of the surface.

Watch your head on these stairs, said the man ahead of me.

Hello Doc, said a boy of about ten coming to my side at the moment. What you here for?

Well, Sonny, why aren't you in school?

I got to stay home and take care of my mother.

Isn't your father here?

Yeah, he's here now. He kept woggling his head, looking down at the floor then up at me with a silly sly expression to his face, swinging his arms around the while as if it might be a clown imitating a monkey. I took up my satchel and leaving him started to climb the stairs, remembering just in time to bow my head so as not to hit the back of the opening above. All short people in this house, I could see that.

At the top of the steep stairway, which merely went up from a corner of the kitchen through the ceiling and landed you in the middle of the bedroom above—I came out between two large iron double beds standing there as if they had been two boats floating in a small docking space, no carpet, no other furniture. Seeing no one I went through the only door to the other room, at the back. These two rooms comprised the whole upstairs.

Here y'are, Doc.

There she lay, in another double iron bed backed against a window. She seemed quite comfortable and rather amused at that. You could see her form, not unattractive, under the old quilt and above it on the pillow a blonde head with a somewhat scarred pointed face. A young woman, Polish in appearance, looking at me, half-smiling.

Well, what's going on?

She's having a lot of pain, Doc. She was five months along and scalded herself on Sunday pretty bad. The pains started yesterday morning.

Here it comes again! she said as we men stood like a

couple of goofs watching her while her face got red and she gritted her teeth and closed her eyes tight for a moment or two.

How often do they come? I asked her after she had relaxed again.

Oh, every few minutes. They're not so bad. But he, indicating her husband, thought he'd better get somebody. We don't know what it is.

You know what it is, I said.

Yeah, I suppose so. But what's this I got here? She put her hand to her lower abdomen. I thought it might be a tumor or something.

Let's see. Why, that's just the womb. You know, I said.

I don't know nothin', she came back at me. Anyhow I wanted you to see it. Then she looked at me with a half smile on her face. You don't recognize me, do you?

No.

You brought one of the children, the first one, ten years ago when we were living down at the Hill.

You don't mean it.

Sure. Don't you remember? Naw, you don't remember. When do you think it'll come, this one, I mean?

I didn't want to bother you, Doc, broke in the man. I'm used to these things but it began to look pretty bad.

How many children you got?

Four. All boys.

This one was supposed to be a girl, said the woman smiling broadly.

Then she began to have another pain and everything stopped for a moment. We watched her until her features gradually relaxed again. It didn't last long but I could see now that she really meant business.

Say, these are coming pretty fast, I said to them. Before we get stuck here let's take a look at that burn.

All right. She threw the covers carelessly down again exposing her thin, well-formed body almost to the knees.

There was an oblong piece of folded cotton rag covering the length of the left thigh, held loosely in place by narrow adhesive strips above and below. I loosened one side of the lower strip and saw the burned area. It must have been a foot long with a big, half-shriveled blister in the center as big as the palm of your hand. I replaced the bandage. We'll leave that alone. Does it hurt much?

Nothing to it. She seemed completely at ease lying there, with none of the deformity apparent that you'd find in a maternity case at term, like a well woman who might be feigning—in all her soiled sheets. Her color was good. She didn't seem greatly concerned about anything—and she was not unattractive! I remarked it again. It was odd to see that rather amused expression on her face. Whom did she remind me of? Oh yes, the woggle-headed kid downstairs. Clowns, the two of them.

I guess it's a good thing, she said. We got enough already.

How much are you getting? said the man to me at that moment.

Are you working?

Yeah, I get eighteen dollars a week but I haven't had more than three days recently.

What do you do?

I work for a house-wrecking company.

Is that so! Well, that's interesting. I thought of what Floss had said. I want to hear more about that later.

I can tell you anything you want to know. How much is it gonna be, Doc?

Well, I said, I don't know. Infection, hemorrhage. That sort of thing; she'll need a little watching. How about ten dollars?

O.K. I'll get you some money. What else do you need?

Nothing I won't have with me.

Don't you want to examine her, Doc?

I don't think so.

But suppose it's coming.

All right, I said. Let's see where we're at. I made a quick examination. The outlet was still contracted; it didn't take me long. The man looked at me as I turned away in mild astonishment.

Is that all?

That's enough for now. She's all right. She's going to have it. It's too bad but it can't be helped. Leave this basin just as it is. I'll be back in about half an hour, just as soon as I can make it.

All right, he answered. I got to walk down to the plant and get some money, it'll take me about that time to get back here too. I'll get the other things. But you'll be back sure, Doc, won't you? You won't not come back, will you? I'll have the money. I won't have it all but I'll have a couple of dollars.

Yeah. And if anything happens while we're gone, I turned to the woman, you just stay where you are, don't get up, don't touch anything. Just stay put. You understand.

I know. All right.

In half an hour I was back at the house again, as agreed. There was an old black-and-white cat lying in the sunny doorway who literally had to be lifted and pushed away before I could enter. As I shoved him off with my foot and kicked open the door—the boy came out from a sort of cubbyhole closet behind the stove, staring.

Oh! he said with wide eyes. You here again? and he looked down at the two bags I was now carrying, one in either hand. You scared me! I thought it was some man pushed open the door to let the cat in. I noticed then that he was wearing a cowboy belt with a large-size snapper pistol in it. One can imagine what he must have been thinking.

Two bags! he said with amazed emphasis. How many times you coming here?

How's your mother?

Oh, she's all right.

Get that cat out. It had followed me into the room.

Get out! he yelled and closed the door behind the slink-
ing beast.

I took my time to look around a bit as I stood there wondering. The whole place had a curious excitement about it
for me, resembling in that the woman herself, I couldn't precisely tell why. There was nothing properly recognizable,
nothing straight, nothing in what ordinarily might have
been called its predictable relationships. Complete disorder.
Tables, chairs, worn-out shoes piled in one corner. A range
that didn't seem to be lighted. Every angle of the room
jammed with something or other ill-assorted and of the
rarest sort.

I have seldom seen such disorder and brokenness—such a
mass of unrelated parts of things lying about. That's it! I
concluded to myself. An unrecognizable order! Actually—
the new! And so good-natured and calm. So definitely the
thing! And so compact. Excellent. And with such patina of
use. Everything definitely "painty." Even the table, that
way, pushed off from the center of the room.

What you gonna do to my mother? the boy asked.

Your father come back yet?

No. What you gonna do?

Just fix her up a bit, I said. I understand you got four
boys in the family. No girls at all?

No girls except my mother.

That's right.

Upstairs again, through the bare bedroom. She looked
just the same.

Anything happen?

Not yet. The pains seem to be getting worse, that's all.

I sat on the edge of the bed to wait. You haven't had any
chills have you?

So quiet, so lovely, so peaceful in that room. So strangely
comforting. I couldn't make it out. Now the woman had
another pain. I watched her.

They been coming that way right along?

About like that.

I sat at the foot of the bed while we talked and waited.

What's all that fluffy stuff on the screen? I said turning to the window.

Yeah, I was wondering about that too, said the woman.

Oh, I see, it's from the meadows, cat-tail down. That wind we had the other day must have blown it up here, quite a distance, isn't it?

When the husband came in with his supplies I removed my coat and took out my light rubber apron.

Now the butcher work begins! she smiled.

There wasn't much change in the situation. So the husband gave me the four dollars he had for me and we fell to talking of the house-wrecking job.

Can't you give her something to ease the pain a little, Doc? said the man.

Sure, if she wants it. These aren't very strong but they may give her a little relief. Just leave everything else the same. I got to get some lunch now, then I have office hours. After that I'll be back, around three o'clock, if you don't call me sooner.

How's it going? said Floss a half hour later.

Just a five months' miss. She's all right.

What sort of people are they?

You can imagine.

Are they going to pay you.

Yes, he gave me four dollars. Said he'd bring me some more when he had it. By the way, here's something interesting, he's a house-wrecker. What do you know about that?

Well?

It's an idea, isn't it?

Didn't I tell you something would come of it? What did he say?

Oh, I didn't get much chance to talk to him but he said they do go out of the state if it's worth their while.

Did you tell him about the stone construction?

He said that don't make no difference. They'll level that off and even fill in the cellar if you have to have it that way. I'll ask him more about it when I get back.

When's it coming off?

I dunno.

What a day! There was the old cat, as before, obstructing the doorway. I felt as though I lived in the place and had lived there always. Inside, the boy was lying on the floor playing with a half-busted mechanical engine and cars. He didn't stir this time or even look up at me. I had to walk over his legs to get to the chair with my coat. Not a sound. Where's your father?

He's upstairs.

I ducked my head instinctively this time. As it came above the flooring into the bedroom above the man got up suddenly from where he had been sleeping on one of the children's beds, rubbing his eyes to open them. He was half-dazed as I walked past him into the woman's labor room. She too had been asleep, opened her eyes and smiled. Marvelous!

I must have been asleep, she said stretching and smiling pleasantly at me.

What's happened to the pains? I said.

It must have been those pills. I had to take them twice but after that the pains left me.

I heard a commotion downstairs, then a grand stampede and clambering on the wooden stairway. Get out of here! I heard the father say loudly. Go on, the whole bunch of youse. Go downstairs. I had to go to look. There they were, all four of them, the three youngest fresh from school, standing around the stairhead like so many pegs, in amazement. I'm hungry, one of them said. Go on, get downstairs. I'll get you something later. But he had to take them bodily, one at a time, and push them ahead of him before he could get them below.

What do you say, Doc? She all right?

Sure, leave her alone.

Am I sleepy, he said. Up all night and doing the cooking and taking care of her. I'm dead. I sat down beside the woman and felt her pulse.

Are you gonna examine me again? she said. No. That's good. I'll come back when it gets ready.

Sure everything's all right, Doc? Those must be good pills you gave her.

Looks like it. Even put you to sleep without taking them, huh? Have you bled any? to the woman.

No, nothing much. I feel good.

All right. I guess then I'd better move on. I got work to do. Call me when you need me—and don't make it four-thirty A.M.

We don't want to bother you, Doc. I'll watch her and let you know when it's coming.

Say, about that wrecking business: How much does it cost to take a house down like I told you.

They'll give you a hundred dollars maybe or if somebody else is bidding maybe they'll make it a hundred and a quarter. It won't cost you nothin'. Have you got a card with you? I'll have the boss see you in your office.

We've got a house eating up seven hundred dollars a year taxes, and nothing coming in. Belongs to my mother-in-law.

Yeah, you can't keep that up.

The kids were waiting for me with open mouths at the foot of the stairs. I rumpled the heavy blond head of hair of one of them and all smiled delightedly following me with their eyes as I said so-long to the father and disappeared from them through the door.

It was four-thirty the next morning when the phone finally rang. Four-thirty! Of course. Aw right, aw right.

It's here, came the voice back at me. Take your time. She can wait till you come.

These are the great neglected hours of the day, the only time when the world is relatively perfect and at peace. But terror guards them. Once I am up, however, and out it's rather a delight, no matter what the weather, to be abroad in the thoughtful dawn.

He was waiting for me in the semi-dark, in his shirt-sleeves, at the curb, and we went in together.

Upstairs the four kids were asleep in the big beds. Two were lying across the one at the right, their heads all but hanging over the edge nearest me, side by side. The older boys were on the other bed, the head of one near the feet of the other. There was no cover on any of them and all were only partially undressed, as if sleep had overtaken them in the act of removing their clothes.

Good for you, I said to the woman. Did you have strong pains?

Yeah, all night but as long as I knew it was all right I could stand it.

It's still in the sack, he said. It all came together.

He was right, the whole mass was intact. Through the thin walls of the membranes the fetus could be plainly made out. About five months.

Is it alive? he asked me.

No.

It was alive when it was born though, she said. I looked and I could see it open its mouth like it wanted to breathe. What is it, Doc, she continued, a boy or a girl?

Oh, boy! said the husband, have I got a bellyache tonight. She laughed. Guess he's having a baby. He's worse than I am.

I feel like it, he said.

Maybe you are, I told him as we started to work over the woman to make her comfortable.

You'd be more famous than the Dionne quintuplets, she smiled. You'd get your pictures in the papers and talk over the radio and everything. Say, Doc, she continued, you haven't told me. What was it?

What do you want to know for?

I want to know if it's a girl.

I looked. Yes, it would have been a girl.

There, she said, you see! Now you've got your girl. I hope you're satisfied.

I haven't got any girl, he answered her quietly.

I'm hungry, yelled a sleepy voice from the other room. Shut up! said the father.

The Practice (from The Autobiography)

IT'S THE HUMDRUM, day-in, day-out, everyday work that is the real satisfaction of the practice of medicine; the million and a half patients a man has seen on his daily visits over a forty-year period of weekdays and Sundays that make up his life. I have never had a money practice; it would have been impossible for me. But the actual calling on people, at all times and under all conditions, the coming to grips with the intimate conditions of their lives, when they were being born, when they were dying, watching them die, watching them get well when they were ill, has always absorbed me.

I lost myself in the very properties of their minds: for the moment at least I actually became *them*, whoever they should be, so that when I detached myself from them at the end of a half-hour of intense concentration over some illness which was affecting them, it was as though I were re-awakening from a sleep. For the moment I myself did not exist, nothing of myself affected me. As a consequence I came back to myself, as from any other sleep, rested.

Time after time I have gone out into my office in the evening feeling as if I couldn't keep my eyes open a moment longer. I would start out on my morning calls after only a few hours' sleep, sit in front of some house waiting to get the courage to climb the steps and push the front-door bell. But once I saw the patient all that would disappear. In a flash the details of the case would begin to formulate themselves into a recognizable outline, the diagnosis would unravel itself, or would refuse to make itself plain, and the hunt was on. Along with that the patient himself would shape up into something that called for attention, his peculiarities, her reticences or candors. And though I might be attracted or repelled, the professional attitude which every physician must call on would steady me, dictate the terms on which I was to proceed. Many a time a man must watch the patient's mind as it watches him, distrusting him, ready to fly off at a tangent at the first opportunity; sees himself distrusted, sees the patient turn to someone else, rejecting him.

More than once we have all seen ourselves rejected, seen some hard-pressed mother or husband go to some other adviser when we know that the advice we have given him has been correct. That too is part of the game. But in general it is the rest, the peace of mind that comes from adopting the patient's condition as one's own to be struggled with toward a solution during those few minutes or that hour or those trying days when we are searching for causes, trying to relate this to that to build a reasonable basis for action which really gives us our peace. As I say, often after I have gone into my office harassed by personal perplexities of whatever sort, fatigued physically and mentally, after two hours of intense application to the work, I came out at the finish completely rested (and I mean rested) ready to smile and to laugh as if the day were just starting.

That is why as a writer I have never felt that medicine interfered with me but rather that it was my very food and drink, the very thing which made it possible for me to write. Was I not interested in man? There the thing was, right in front of me. I could touch it, smell it. It was myself, naked, just as it was, without a lie telling itself to me in its own terms. Oh, I knew it wasn't for the most part giving me anything very profound, but it was giving me terms, basic terms with which I could spell out matters as profound as I cared to think of.

I knew it was an elementary world that I was facing, but I have always been amazed at the authenticity with which the simple-minded often face that world when compared with the tawdriness of the public viewpoint exhibited in reports from the world at large. The public view which affects the behavior of so many is a very shabby thing when compared with what I see every day in my practice of medicine. I can almost say it is the interference of the public view of their lives with what I see which makes the difficulty, in most instances, between sham and a satisfactory basis of thought.

I don't care much about that, however. I don't care a rap what people are or believe. They come to me. I care for them and either they become my friends or they don't. That is their business. My business, aside from the mere physical diagnosis, is to make a different sort of diagnosis concerning them as individuals, quite apart from anything for which they seek my advice. That fascinates me. From the very beginning that fascinated me even more than I myself knew. For no matter where I might find myself, every sort of individual that it is possible to imagine in some phase of his development, from the highest to the lowest, at some time exhibited himself to me. I am sure I have seen them all. And all have contributed to my pie. Let the successful carry off their blue ribbons; I have known the unsuccessful, far better persons than their more lucky brothers. One can laugh at them both, whatever the costumes they adopt. And when one is able to reveal them to themselves, high or low, they are always grateful as they are surprised that one can so have revealed the inner secrets of another's private motives. To do this is what makes a writer worth heeding: that somehow or other, whatever the source may be, he has gone to the base of the matter to lay it bare before us in terms which, try as we may, we cannot in the end escape. There is no choice then but to accept him and make him a hero.

All day long the doctor carries on this work, observing,

weighing, comparing values of which neither he nor his patients may know the significance. He may be insensitive. But if in addition to actually being an accurate craftsman and a man of insight he has the added quality of—some distress of mind, a restless concern with the . . . If he is not satisfied with mere cures, if he lacks ambition, if he is content to . . . If there is no content in him and likely to be none; if in other words, without wishing to force it, since that would interfere with his lifelong observation, he allows himself to be called a name! What can one think of him?

He is half-ashamed to have people suspect him of carrying on a clandestine, a sort of underhand piece of spying on the public at large. They naively ask him, "How do you do it? How can you carry on an active business like that and at the same time find time to write? You must be superhuman. You must have at the very least the energy of two men." But they do not grasp that one occupation complements the other, that they are two parts of a whole, that it is not two jobs at all, that one rests the man when the other fatigues him. The only person to feel sorry for is his wife. She practically becomes a recluse. His only fear is that the source of his interest, his daily going about among human beings of all sorts, all ages, all conditions will be terminated. That he will be found out.

As far as the writing itself is concerned it takes next to no time at all. Much too much is written every day of our lives. We are overwhelmed by it. But when at times we see through the welter of evasive or interested patter, when by chance we penetrate to some moving detail of a life, there is always time to bang out a few pages. The thing isn't to find the time for it—we waste hours every day doing absolutely nothing at all—the difficulty is to catch the evasive life of the thing, to phrase the words in such a way that stereotype will yield a moment of insight. That is where the difficulty lies. We are lucky when that underground current can be tapped and the secret spring of all our lives will send up its pure water. It seldom happens. A thousand trivialities push themselves to the front, our lying habits of everyday speech and thought are foremost, telling us that *that* is what "they" want to hear. Tell them something else. You know you want to be a successful writer. This sort of chitchat the daily practice of medicine tends drastically to cure.

Forget writing, it's a trivial matter. But day in day out, when the inarticulate patient struggles to lay himself bare for you, or with nothing more than a boil on his back is so caught off balance that he reveals some secret twist of a whole community's pathetic way of thought, a man is suddenly seized again with a desire to speak of the underground stream which for a moment has come up just under the surface. It is just a glimpse, an intimation of all that which the daily print misses or deliberately hides, but the excitement is intense and the rush to write is on again. It is then we see, by this constant feeling for a meaning, from the unselected nature of the material, just as it comes in over the phone or at the office door, that there is no better way to get an intimation of what is going on in the world.

We catch a glimpse of something, from time to time, which shows us that a presence has just brushed past us, some rare thing—just when the smiling little Italian woman has left us. For a moment we are dazzled. What was that? We can't name it; we know it never gets into any recognizable avenue of expression; men will be long dead before they can have so much as ever approached it. Whole lives are spent in the tremendous affairs of daily events without even approaching the great sights that I see every day. My patients do not know what is about them among their very husbands and children, their wives and acquaintances. But there is no need for us to be such strangers to each other, saving alone laziness, indifference and age-old besotted ignorance.

So for me the practice of medicine has become the pursuit of a rare element which may appear at any time, at any

place, at a glance. It can be most embarrassing. Mutual recognition is likely to flare up at a moment's notice. The relationship between physician and patient, if it were literally
followed, would give us a world of extraordinary fertility
of the imagination which we can hardly afford. There's no
use trying to multiply cases, it is there, it is magnificent, it
fills my thoughts, it reaches to the farthest limits of our
lives.

What is the use of reading the common news of the day,
the tragic deaths and abuses of daily living, when for over
half a lifetime we have known that they must have occurred
just as they have occurred given the conditions that cause
them? There is no light in it. It is trivial fill-gap. We know
the plane will crash, the train be derailed. And we know
why. No one cares, no one can care. We get the news and
discount it, we are quite right in doing so. It is trivial. But
the hunted news I get from some obscure patients' eyes is
not trivial. It is profound: whole academies of learning,
whole ecclesiastical hierarchies are founded upon it and
have developed what they call their dialectic upon nothing
else, their lying dialectics. A dialectic is any arbitrary system, which, since all systems are mere inventions, is neces-
sarily in each case a false premise, upon which a closed system is built shutting those who confine themselves to it from
the rest of the world. All men one way or another use a
dialectic of some sort into which they are shut, whether it
be an Argentina or a Japan. So each group is maimed. Each
is enclosed in a dialectic cloud, incommunicado, and for that
reason we rush into wars and prides of the most superficial
natures.

Do we not see that we are inarticulate? That is what defeats us. It is our inability to communicate to another how
we are locked within ourselves, unable to say the simplest
thing of importance to one another, any of us, even the
most valuable, that makes our lives like those of a litter of
kittens in a wood-pile. That gives the physician, and I don't

mean the high-priced psychoanalyst, his opportunity; psychoanalysis amounts to no more than another dialectic into which to be locked.

The physician enjoys a wonderful opportunity actually to witness the words being born. Their actual colors and shapes are laid before him carrying their tiny burdens which he is privileged to take into his care with their unspoiled newness. He may see the difficulty with which they have been born and what they are destined to do. No one else is present but the speaker and ourselves, we have been the words' very parents. Nothing is more moving.

But after we have run the gamut of the simple meanings that come to one over the years, a change gradually occurs. We have grown used to the range of communication which is likely to reach us. The girl who comes to me breathless, staggering into my office, in her underwear a still breathing infant, asking me to lock her mother out of the room; the man whose mind is gone—all of them finally say the same thing. And then a new meaning begins to intervene. For under that language to which we have been listening all our lives a new, a more profound language, underlying all the dialectics offers itself. It is what they call poetry. That is the final phase.

It is that, we realize, which beyond all they have been saying is what they have been trying to say. They laugh (For are they not laughable?); they can think of nothing more useless (What else are they but the same?); something made of words (Have they not been trying to use words all their lives?). We begin to see that the underlying meaning of all they want to tell us and have always failed to communicate is the poem, the poem which their lives are being lived to realize. No one will believe it. And it is the actual words, as we hear them spoken under all circumstances, which contain it. It is actually there, in the life before us, every minute that we are listening, a rarest element—not in our imaginations but there, there in fact. It is that essence which is hidden in the very words which are going in at our ears and from which we must recover underlying meaning as realistically as we recover metal out of ore.

The poem that each is trying actually to communicate to us lies in the words. It is at least the words that make it articulate. It has always been so. Occasionally that named person is born who catches a rumor of it, a Homer, a Villon, and his race and the world perpetuates his memory. Is it not plain why? The physician, listening from day to day, catches a hint of it in his preoccupation. By listening to the minutest variations of the speech we begin to detect that today, as always, the essence is also to be found, hidden under the verbiage, seeking to be realized.

But one of the characteristics of this rare presence is that it is jealous of exposure and that it is shy and revengeful. It is not a name that is bandied about in the market place, no more than it is something that can be captured and exploited by the academy. Its face is a particular face, it is likely to appear under the most unlikely disguises. You cannot recognize it from past appearances—in fact it is always a new face. It knows all that we are in the habit of describing. It will not use the same appearance for any new materialization. And it is our very life. It is we ourselves, at our rarest moments, but inarticulate for the most part except when in the poem one man, every five or six hundred years, escapes to formulate a few gifted sentences.

The poem springs from the half-spoken words of such patients as the physician sees from day to day. He observes it in the peculiar, actual conformations in which its life is hid. Humbly he presents himself before it and by long practice he strives as best he can to interpret the manner of its speech. In that the secret lies. This, in the end, comes perhaps to be the occupation of the physician after a lifetime of careful listening.

The Birth

A 40 odd year old Para 10
        Navarra
              or Navatta she didn't know
uncomplaining
        in the little room
              where we had been working all night long
dozing off
        by 10 or 15 minute intervals
             her great pendulous belly
marked
        by contraction rings
            under the skin.
No progress.
It was restfully quiet
        approaching dawn on Guinea Hill
            in those days.
Wha's a ma', Doc?
        It do'n wanna come.
That finally roused me.
I got me a strong sheet
        wrapped it
            tight
around her belly.
        When the pains seized her again
            the direction
was changed
        not
            against her own backbone

but downward
            toward the exit.
                        It began to move — stupid
not to have thought of that earlier.
Finally
            without a cry out of her
                        more than a low animal moaning
the head emerged
            up to the neck.
It took its own time
            rotating.
I thought of a good joke
            about an infant
                        at that moment of its career
and smiled to myself quietly
            behind my mask.
                        I am a feminist.
After a while
            I was able
                        to extract the shoulders
one at a time
            a tight fit.
                        Madonna!
13½ pounds!
            Not a man among us
                        can have equaled
that.

Le Médecin Malgré Lui

Oh I suppose I should
wash the walls of my office
polish the rust from
my instruments and keep them
definitely in order
build shelves in the laboratory
empty out the old stains
clean the bottles
and refill them, buy
another lens, put
my journals on edge instead of
letting them lie flat
in heaps—then begin
ten years back and
gradually
read them to date
cataloguing important
articles for ready reference.
I suppose I should
read the new books.
If to this I added
a bill at the tailor's
and at the cleaner's
grew a decent beard
and cultivated a look
of importance—
Who can tell? I might be
a credit to my Lady Happiness
and never think anything
but a white thought!

Dead Baby

Sweep the house
    under the feet of the curious
    holiday seekers—
sweep under the table and the bed
    the baby is dead—

The mother's eyes where she sits
   by the window, unconsoled—
have purple bags under them
    the father—
tall, wellspoken, pitiful
    is the abler of these two—

Sweep the house clean
    here is one who has gone up
    (though problematically)
to heaven, blindly
    by force of the facts—
a clean sweep
    is one way of expressing it—

Hurry up! any minute
    they will be bringing it
    from the hospital—
a white model of our lives
    a curiosity—
    surrounded by fresh flowers

A Cold Front

This woman with a dead face
has seven foster children
and a new baby of her own in
spite of that. She wants pills

for an abortion and says,
Un hum, in reply to me while
her blanketed infant makes
unrelated grunts of salutation.

She looks at me with her mouth
open and blinks her expressionless
carved eyes, like a cat
on a limb too tired to go higher

from its tormentors. And still
the baby chortles in its spit
and there is a dull flush
almost of beauty to the woman's face

as she says, looking at me
quietly, I won't have any more.
In a case like this I know
quick action is the main thing.

The Poor

By constantly tormenting them
with reminders of the lice in
their children's hair, the
School Physician first
brought their hatred down on him.
But by this familiarity
they grew used to him, and so,
at last,
took him for their friend and adviser.

To Close

Will you please rush down and see
ma baby. You know, the one I talked
to you about last night

What was that?

Is this the baby specialist?

Yes, but perhaps you mean my son,
can't you wait until   .   ?

I, I, I, don't think it's brEAthin'

Afterword: My Father, the Doctor

. . . how I do long for a full expression of everything that is in me, a free outpouring of everything I feel. I have patience, I have love of men and women and children and trees—I can watch over a thing for years—in fact forever and nurse it into its full strength, but there is still a part of me that yearns for the unknown perfection—not a religious, heavenly perfection but a full-blooded earthly perfection that is fragile as all life is and as sweet.

Writing to his mother in the spring of 1916, my father sounds like anything but a struggling young physician, three years married, father of one, still being judged by the established physicians of the town, as well as a school doctor and physician to the county orphanage, serving gratis. In his freshman year at the University of Pennsylvania Medical School, he had established in his own mind that his love lay in the arts, but he would persist with his medical education for the income it would bring, thus making possible the pursuit of his muse. And his practice of medicine, like all things he would undertake, would be a full-time job, conscientiously pursued, the need of his patient always receiving first priority. As if to apologize to the art of medicine for placing it second to poetry in his favor, he would go to the front lines, the trenches where the truly needy were, taking with him his knowledge and skill. He would become what we now know as a family practitioner.

This double commitment, to poetry and to medicine, would dictate his manner of living for the rest of his life. It

133

demanded time and energy, and he would supply both bountifully, often at the expense of his family. Here at home we experienced a daily countdown and "blast off." By the time we assembled for breakfast, he had probably already done an hour's stint on the typewriter. There was no physicians' exchange—the phone was at his elbow at mealtimes, brought to the table on an extension cord. Another interruption was the mailman's whistle, announcing the morning delivery of mail. (A second delivery would come at one o'clock.) The list of calls having been compiled, he was out the door to the garage before we kids had swallowed our cod-liver oil and lit out for school. First stop probably the post office, mailing manuscripts and personal correspondence to maintain communication with his fellow poets, and in later years to advise the young ones aspiring to recognition. Then house calls, working his way to the hospital for rounds, clinics, committee meetings, whatnot. Finally home for lunch, a sit-down meal, hopefully twenty to thirty minutes allowed for nourishment and conversation with Floss. Often a quick nap on the couch in the living room, then one o'clock office hours, conducted for forty years without nurse or secretary assistance—a small attached lab for basic blood and urine analyses—one to three p.m., or until the last patient was seen. House calls again, particularly in winter, with perhaps fifteen minutes swiped to get down a fragment of verse on the machine folded away beneath the office desk. Evening and supper waiting. Mom frequently telling Lucy, the maid, to put it on the table for herself and us two boys and a plate in the oven for the doctor. Home to eat. Napkin folded, rolled and tucked in its ring before the retreat through the kitchen to the office again. Once more hours seven to nine, or until the last patient was seen, hating this ultimate drain on his time and energy, as he would confess years later to Ezra Pound. "I am now engaged in cutting out much of my medical work under the guise of becoming a 'specialist.' Within a few months I will have done with evening office hours, that hellish drag."

Where in this hectic daily routine was there time for poetry? Where would he find energy and peace of mind to give "a free outpouring of everything I feel"? Where would he find "the unknown perfection—not a religious, heavenly perfection but a full-blooded earthly perfection that is fragile as all life is and as sweet"? Part of the answer lies in his great opportunism—the talent for grasping, creating precious moments stolen from that alter ego, the doctor, and used to unburden himself of poetic images. Perhaps on the road to the hospital, the car would be drawn to the curb and a fragment jotted awkwardly in pencil in a little red notebook which started life as a record of his doings as school doctor, and latterly became a catchall for images, phrases, and poems, such as:

When I glance
from the
colored ad of
Min's
corsets to the
healthy
creature sitting
below it
then I realize
at last the
sacredness of art

But then
continuing home
from the opera
I enjoy the
walk under
the trees in the
cool more—
which proves
art to be
futile.

Alternating notes concerning school business and writing continue page after page:

Sept. 10 Visited all schools

Sept. 14 Visited all schools and began
exam. Wash. and Union.

Meany-Mumps
tel. Thomas

Sept. 15 Excl. L———'s 3 children
Sylvan impetigo till Monday.

31 in Wash. Kindergart.—*Too many*

This is obviously the notebook of a conscientious school physician, and for the first four pages all entries concern school matters. Suddenly on page 4:

what is it that is so excellent in the Japanese artist? but that they have seen their fish, their fowls, their horses in intimate completeness.

Then more pages of school business.

Sept. 29 6th grade Pierrepont School
exam for pediculosis
One exclud. Marie D———

Lincoln
No way to turn off room
—Pipes in Kind. covered c asbestos

Interjections irrelevant to school business increase. Finally the little notebook has been reversed, and the rear pages used exclusively for images, sketches, and quotations from the speech of patients.

The little red notebook will record the details of the nit-picking daily drudgery of the school doctor and help him make his report to the Board of Health. But it will also catch and hold like a Breughel canvas the human parade, the chips and flakes that fly about for the sensitive mind to appreciate and harvest. Here is a handwritten record of the workings of the mind of a poet-physician on his daily rounds, including, further along, this prescription for himself:

If I did not have
    verse
I would have died
or been
a thief

But even larger chunks of time were available while the rest of the world slept. It was at night that he would call on apparently endless stores of energy, the tattoo of his type-writer providing a reassuring lullaby to which my brother Paul and I slept and awoke throughout childhood. I can recall the projection of his mood brought to me by the cadence of the keys—the smooth andante when all was happy and serene, and the interrupted staccato when the going got rough, the carriage slamming, and the paper ripped from the roller, balled, and heaved in the direction of the waste-basket. Night was his time to roar. Here was happiness, his love, Poetry, but apparently in insufficient quantity or quality to completely satisfy. Further along in his letter to his mother he will say: "I must do something . . . some high deed of spiritual happiness, nothing cowardly, nothing low, nothing small—some deed of great love for humanity perhaps, some venture for the sake of poetry, the art I love." And in another paragraph, "I must dare higher. It is only the (?) fire we ourselves put into our lives that gives strength to our imaginations, it is the power of love that makes us live and do. Just as at Penn I gave up dentistry for medicine—just as a little later I really gave up medicine for poetry—and a little later I gave up a personal disappointment and its bitterness for dearest Flossie's love and the care of it so now I feel on the brink of a new change."

Here is a man making his living at medicine who has given up medicine for poetry. One wonders how he originally became involved in the medical process. Being an inexact science, medicine would certainly be no medium for this man of strongly idealistic philosophy to employ in his search for the "unknown perfection," whatever that might be. Undoubtedly there were parental forces that determined what his role in life would be. The strongest influence in his home environment was his mother, if only because she was continually present while his traveling papa was elsewhere for the greatest part of the formative years of both Will and his brother, Ed. His mother's brother Carlos, a Paris-educated physician, was the apple of Elena's eye, and her total support after the death of her parents. He had returned from France to their home in Puerto Rico, later moving to Santo Domingo, and finally with his sister safely married to my grandfather, migrated to the mainland, first to Panama and later to Ecuador. Young Will was impressed by Mama, with whom as man and boy he always maintained a very close spiritual relationship, to continue the "tradition" and become a physician. "Pop" the wandering agent, on the other hand, having a very fuzzy familial anlage which *his* mother, Grandma Welcome, would never divulge, certainly could bring no pressure based on family precedent. He was, however, a drug salesman on a grand scale. Apparently his whole professional life was devoted to one concern, a wholesale supplier and importer of medicinals, Lanman and Kemp, 137 Water Street, New York City, founded A.D. 1808. This required travel to cities as widely separated and disparate as Geneva and Guayaquil, which was no small accomplishment and kept him away from home for months at a time. (There was very little express air travel to Europe and South America be-

tween 1880 and 1918, when he died.) What type of agent
he was, and how familiar with medical terminology he was,
I don't know, but as an indicator of some of the literature
he was familiar with, I quote from a letter he wrote to my
father on April 27, 1906. "I mailed you yesterday what I
think you will find a good book, consisting of extracts from
Dr. Osler's writings. . . . I read an article lately, from the
London *Lancet* I think, in which it said that it is a fallacy to
suppose that an unlimited amount of menial work can be
done if an equal excess of physical exercise is performed."

So we have an English gentleman papa (he never became
an American citizen), who is to some extent conversant
with medical literature, apparently for business purposes.
Somehow I doubt this was ever a factor in my father's de-
cision to become a physician. On the other hand I feel
Mama leaned heavily on her son Will to emulate his Uncle
Carlos. She got her wish and thereby initiated a dichotomy
in his life which persisted until in late years a series of cere-
bral and neoplastic illnesses made it impossible for him to
continue either as artist or physician.

During his productive years he had frequently flirted
with the idea of giving up medicine and seeking his living as
a writer. His friend Ezra Pound had urged him to pull up
stakes and go to Europe, where the action was, and he and
Floss made two trips to France, Austria, and Italy in the
twenties, sampling the Bohemian life of the artists in Paris
and living for a while on the Riviera. On their first trip just
after World War I they went to Vienna, where Dad studied
in the clinics of what were then some of the leading lights
in the beginning specialty of pediatrics. It was on his return
to the States after this experience that he began to limit his
practice more and more to the diseases of children. However, the dream of the artist's life never materialized. It must
have been obvious to him that the public was not ready for
his work: "Gee Doc, your poetry is very interesting, but
what does it mean?" For which he had no answer, main-

taining that if the poem had no significance to the reader on
first reading, there was little hope that interpretation by the
author would give any more profound enlightenment.

I recall a reading one evening at the home of a local physician, the audience consisting entirely of fellow doctors
from his hospital. Gentlemen all. Fond of old Doctor Bill.
Polite and attentive, aware of his reputation as a poet, anx-
ious to get the word, *i.e.* the key to the code that would
make it all clear. . . . His closing lines were much in the
form and mood of an orison.

> O clemens! O pia! O dolcis!
> Maria!

There was an appropriate silence at the conclusion, broken
after ten or fifteen seconds by the host, who inquired, "Are
you a Catholic, Bill?" To which Dad replied in the negative,
adding that so far as formal religion went, he was brought
up a Unitarian, though his parents had been Catholic and
Church of England. It was immediately apparent to me that
he was perturbed about something, although it wasn't until
later driving home that he could explain his annoyance to
me, *i.e.*, the inference that his spontaneous expression of love
and respect for some power beyond our understanding
must stem from some formal catechism dictating his
thoughts and emotions. However, there was nothing vin-
dictive in his reaction, for by this stage in his life he had
grown to accept his eccentricity and his designation as a
revolutionary in the arts.

It was a more painful experience to be rebuffed by his
brother Ed. The two boys were born within a year of each
other. They had always been pals, commuted together to
Horace Mann for years, played on the same teams (Dad the
pitcher and Ed the catcher), dated the same girls (later each
had his proposal of marriage turned down by the same girl),
were classmates in Switzerland and Paris, corresponded

regularly when Dad was at Penn and Ed at M.I.T., traveled together through Italy in 1910 when Ed was enjoying his reward (studying in Rome) for winning the prestigious Prix de Rome and Dad was returning to his fiancée in Rutherford after a year of postgraduate study in Leipzig. Our home always featured paintings that Ed gave Dad for Christmas. He was a very good watercolorist, and his works didn't suffer by being exhibited on the same walls with Demuth, Sheeler, Hartley, and Shahn. But Ed was a conservative, a student of classical architecture, with no patience for the radical and the *outré*. His attitude toward his brother's work had always been one of smiling understanding and tolerance—give the boy plenty of rope and he'll hang himself sort of thing. But one morning a volume of Dad's poems that he had been at pains to deliver to Ed's home appeared in our mailbox, apparently placed there by Edgar on his daily trip by the house en route to the 7:52 to New York on the Erie. There was an accompanying letter describing the book's contents as vulgar and immoral, incomprehensible balderdash, and something that he, Ed, would not tolerate in his home.

To quote from Chapter 4 of Dad's autobiography, "I'll never forget the dream I had a few days after he [his father] died, after a wasting illness, on Christmas Day 1918. I saw him coming down a peculiar flight of exposed steps, steps I have since identified as those before the dais of Pontius Pilate in some well-known painting. But this was in a New York office building, Pop's office. He was bareheaded and had some business letters in his hand on which he was concentrating as he descended. I noticed him and with joy cried out, 'Pop! so, you're *not* dead!' But he only looked up at me over his right shoulder and commented severely, 'You know all that poetry you're writing. Well, it's no good.' I was left speechless and woke trembling. I have never dreamed of him since."

Misunderstood by the man in the street (whom he dearly

loved), an enigma to his peers in the medical profession, condemned as a blasphemer by his closest pal, his brother, and finally as they say in the vernacular "wiped out" by his father, it becomes fairly obvious why he could never convince himself that there was a living for him to be made in writing. Fortunately there was medicine, his *entrée* into the homes and minds of his neighbors, which qualified him to explore, as he himself put it, the ischio-rectal abcesses of mankind, and incidentally thereby earn a living. The "art" of medicine would be his crutch, supporting him and his family while he was "absent" on his crusade. How successful was his assault on the citadel only he would be qualified to say. Recognition by his contemporaries of a "good try" would come posthumously as the Pulitzer Prize for *Pictures from Brueghel*.

William Eric Williams, M.D.
February 1983
Rutherford, New Jersey

PUBLIC LIBRARY OF BROOKLINE

3 1712 00535 3407

1/85

Public Library of Brookline, Mass.

MAIN LIBRARY
361 Washington Street
Brookline, Mass.   02146

I M P O R T A N T

Leave cards in pocket